THE BOOK OF KATERINA

THE BOOK OF KATERINA

Auguste Corteau

Translated by
Claire Papamichail

PARTHIAN

CYNGOR LLYFRAU CYMRU
BOOKS COUNCIL of WALES

Creative
Europe

Co-funded by the Creative Europe Programme of
the European Union

Auguste Corteau is the pen name of Petros Hatzopoulos. Born in Thessaloniki in 1979, he currently lives in Athens. He is the author of fourteen novels as well as plays, novellas and short story collections and is a recipient of the Greek National Book Award for Children's Literature. He has also translated many works of literature into Greek, from Nabokov's *Lolita* to Cormac McCarthy's *No Country for Old Men*. An LGBT activist, in 2016 he signed a Cohabitation Pact with his partner, the first same-sex couple to do so after the law was passed in the Greek Parliament.

Claire Papamichael was born in Athens, Greece in 1963. She studied Sociology and has been working as a literary translator for more than thirty-five years. Two of the books she translated, *Bleak House* by Charles Dickens and *The Comedians* by Graham Greene, were shortlisted for the National Translation Award and the English-to-Greek Translation Award respectively. She lives in Athens and loves Branston Pickle and clotted cream.

To Puppy, lord and master of my heart

Parthian, Cardigan SA43 1ED
www.parthianbooks.com
First published as Το βιβλίο της Κατερίνας 2013
© S. Patakis S.A & Petros Hatzopoulos Athens 2013
© This translation by Claire Papamichail
ISBN print: 978-1-912681-26-6
ISBN ebook: 978-1-913640-14-9
Editor: Jennifer Barclay
Cover Design: Syncopated Pandemonium
Cover image © Petros Hatzopoulos
Typeset by Elaine Sharples
Printed in EU by 4Edge
Published with the financial support of the Welsh Books Council and the
Creative Europe Programme of the European Union
British Library Cataloguing in Publication Data
A cataloguing record for this book is available from the British Library.

In the desert
I saw a creature, naked, bestial,
Who, squatting upon the ground,
Held his heart in his hands,
And ate of it.
I said: "Is it good, friend?"
"It is bitter—bitter," he answered;
"But I like it
  Because it is bitter,
  And because it is my heart."
                              — *Stephen Crane*

We live in the pit of a hellhole where every
moment is a miracle.
                              — *E.M. Cioran*

III Angels Only

My story begins at the end – both the story's end and my own.

My son found me. Crack of dawn on Friday, five days before he turned twenty-four. He knew right away I was dead, although nothing had changed around the house; maybe because, even in death, I greeted him at the door as always.

It was late December and the radiators were on full blast. I was on the bed, stark naked. I'd put on a lot of weight the last few years, and when I slept both clothes and covers felt suffocating. It was like something from a tragic poem of suffering and love: he was naked when I first saw him and now, the last time he'd ever see me, I was naked too.

After he'd assessed at a glance my deathly state, he turned to the window, thinking whether he should open it – to let the soul of the departed fly away, as they believed in the old days. Something bothered him, though: he didn't want me to catch a chill, lying there stark naked. So he just stood there, immobilised, staring at me.

If I were alive and, upon waking up, found him staring between my big fat thighs, I'd have been terribly ashamed and pull the sheet to cover myself. Yet I was now beyond shame. Also, my son's fixed stare made sense in a way. *That's where I came from,* he thought. *And now...* Now he pictured himself as a leaf, a flower or a fruit brutally wrenched off its branch. For a while, we sat like this and felt the pain together, and then, although he knew he ought to leave me just as he'd found me, totally untouched, he started to tidy me up.

With a wet cloth he wiped the dried bile off my chin and, raising my head on the pillow, he closed my gaping mouth. Then he pushed my legs back together and covered me up with an old sheet, part of my dowry which had sadly outlived me. And these ministrations were as tender as a poem's verses: I used to wipe the drool of his tiny baby's chin in the same way, I used to cover him up in the same way when I woke up early in the morning and found him curled up in his crib without his blanket.

What followed is unimportant. Only those moments, while I lay next to him, unable to put my arms around him and comfort him, and so I merely said, *Cry, my chick. Cry the hurt away*. But it was too soon; it was only an eerie feeling that filled his heart at that moment. He would cry the next day, he would cry years later, he would cry a thousand times as hard as he didn't cry that morning.

And so my story begins. My name is Katerina, and I died by a route dark and lonely, for there was too much in me I could bear no longer. I died terrified and deserted, choking on my own venom. But I don't deserve your pity, so don't pity me. I died by my own hand.

As befits a murderess.

The Cover-Up

It's the dawn of the twentieth century, and in Samsun, Turkey, a silent crime occurs: a woman's past is bluntly erased and so will remain unknown for more than a century. But the fate of this people – *my* people, my son's people – is written with sacrifices and crimes: a palimpsest of hate.

Her name is Sarah, and at the age of twenty-five, poor and unmarried, she is already doomed to spinsterhood. Who would ever marry a Jewess with hair as red as the beard of Judas and without so much as knickers on her arse? And yet, against all odds, Dimitrós Konstantinidis does: an unsuccessful textile merchant, orphaned and thus free of judgmental parents. However, in order to reconcile himself with the fact of wedding a woman who's a year older than him *and* a descendant of Christ-killers into the bargain he asks (or rather *demands;* men rarely *asked* for things in those days) that Sarah forswear her true name and lineage. He might not be rich, but he's a good Christian who crosses himself and fasts during Lent (at least in public) and if he's to have a family with her he won't tolerate her raising his children (sons, that is) to be Christ-killers. And so, without further ado, he renames his bride Katina, takes her by the hand and marries her in front of a handful of people in a remote tiny church.

A married woman now, with a roof over her head, Sarah soon turns into Katina at heart and churns out Dimitrós's brood – although all three children are girls, following one another like stabs in his heart: Irini, Ariadne and Fotini. And as if *that* weren't bad enough, their being dowry-demanding wenches, the wretched things look as different from one another as if they were spawned by the Twelve Tribes: Irini blond and blue-eyed, Ariadne swarthy as a gypsy, and Fotini redheaded and freckled like her mother.

And yet, thanks to Katina's thrifty housekeeping – her unnameable origin had its benefits after all – and industrious Dimitrós working night and day so that his daughters want for nothing, their wealth grows steadily, and at the beginning of the 1920s the Konstantinidis pack is practically well-off: the girls at a good school with piano lessons and foreign languages, meat on the table every day, and thanks be to God.

And then the Asia Minor Catastrophe happens and they suddenly find themselves in Upper Town, Thessaloniki, without two pennies to rub together. Gentleman and businessman

Dimitrós is overnight a spawn of the Turk, and young Irini, who used to be on the top of her class, is suddenly cast amongst smart Greek girls who look down on her and whisper behind her back: "Her family lives in a *shack*. Can you imagine?"

This shack will haunt Irini for the rest of her days. She who wanted to be a doctor when she grew up now crouches by the hearth to warm her freezing hands, while in the pot her dinner of boiled potatoes seethes like her smarting pride ("What's for dinner tonight, sis?" – "Bread and teeth to chew it with"). Moreover, *she* has to cook for the little ones because, as if things weren't bad enough, their mother died just after they emigrated. They took her away in the public horse-drawn cart.

Irini, my mother, quenches her hunger with dreams, while her two younger sisters live in their own private worlds – literally. Although they won't be diagnosed for decades, Fotini, the youngest, suffers from a mild form of mental retardation, while Ariadne – she of the green eyes and the raven-black hair, a beauty sought after by prospective husbands ever since she was twelve – has begun to exhibit the early signs of the paranoid schizophrenia that will plague her till the end of her life.

A lot of hereditary illness in my family; a heavy legacy. As if that first crime (the re-baptism of my Jewish grandmother) was now exacting Biblical vengeance on her innocent girls. But what can you do?

At least Irini is mentally stable – though physically weak. The hardships of her adolescence will cost her a lung lost to consumption and a slight yet persistent hump. Like her late mother, at twenty she'll resemble a grown woman, and so will run into the arms of the first available suitor, preferably one who will be able to restore her to her childhood grandeur.

We were all stricken by the Catastrophe. Our lives were all blighted by that shack.

Father's Malice

In January 1901, my father, Minas Horianos, is born in mountainous Karditsa. Second son, second in everything. The firstborn son, his brother Vangos, has his future laid out before him: school, then studies, and later an illustrious career in the army, where he'll be known by the moniker 'Vangos the Commie-Slayer'. Minas, on the other hand, grows up with barely a rare, stray caress from his Vlach mother Katingo, who spoke no Greek at all. Minas lived like a mute, but with plenty of contempt and corporal punishment from his father, the village priest.

The last bitterness the young Minas is forced to swallow comes in the form of Communion wine – because, in order to remind him just how inferior he is, my ogre of a grandfather makes his own son receive Communion after every other villager, amongst them an old, phthisic woman that Minas despises. And one morning, when he couldn't be older than eight at the time, he knocks the chalice out of his father's hands and says: "May the devil ride your mother!" And with a parting gob of spit in the aghast priest's face, he leaves his homeland forever.

He'll be taken in by a kind-hearted uncle, a pastry maker in Karditsa – although his kindness does not extend to the inside of his home. Little Minas spends the cold winter nights shivering in the henhouse in the yard. And as if this hardship and the backbreaking labour with which he pays for his keep weren't punishment enough, his sleepmates give him chicken lice. For the rest of his life he'll bear these two evils in mind like the two faces of the same beast: every time he sees a priest he'll spit showily on the ground, murmuring: "Go clean the chicken lice from your filthy beard, you motherfucking goat."

The 1920s find him in Thessaloniki at a market stall in Modiano Arcade, peddling balls of yarn, spools of thread, thimbles and other sewing paraphernalia side-by-side with the future magnates of Greece's second-largest city. Working like a dog, he'll make money, and by 1930 he'll be the owner of a large grocery store, almost like a supermarket at that time, which will provide for generations of idlers to come… (The building, unlike its first inhabitants, still stands.)

In 1931, my father Minas will meet my mother Irini, younger by a decade, fall head-over-heels in love with her and marry her. And what about Mrs Irini Horianos? Years later – while confiding to her youngest and most troubled daughter (me), her long-time confidante since, because even if she blabs, who would ever believe crazy Katerina's lies? – when I ask her whether she too had fallen in love with dad, she'll reply after an uncomfortable pause:

"I learnt to love him over the years." As if Minas were a foreign language, which she'd been forced to become fluent in, though she found it hard and uninviting.

Readers, doctor, look no further: therein lies the seed of all evil.

Encephalitis, They Said

In 1933, Dimitris is born – a blond, green-eyed, gorgeous baby. Irini, proud mother and home-maker, already has a cleaner (it's big, that house overlooking the Thermaikos Gulf, and how could she manage the housework alone?), but following her son's birth she also employs an nanny – a distant niece of hers from a village in Roumeli called Zoë – to share some of the maternal burden.

Zoë is an interesting case. The seventh daughter in a row, a few hours after her birth in 1924 she is placed inside a baking tin like an uncooked baby pie and is left up on the roof to freeze to death in the night and free her father from the task of feeding another mouth which will grow into one more dowry-devouring wench. Hearing her weak whine, the village priest will save her, retrieving baby Zoë and raising her with the help of his barren wife as if she were their own.

This feat of salvation will follow Zoë for her entire life like an aura of blessedness and she will share it, along with her tenderness and love. She'll practically raise her aunt Irini's kids all by herself, and even though she'll never have children of her own, she won't ever grow bitter or envious. My son will worship her like a second mother and on the night of her sudden death my brother Agis and I will be jolted out of our sleep, convinced there's been an earthquake.

But let's go back to Dimitris, my brother whom I never met – he died at the age of twenty, a little while after I was born.

During the first three or four years of his life he was an angel, a baby of cherubic beauty and calm: he never cried, nor screamed – he just smiled and smiled, though he was extremely timid and reserved when it came to being kissed, caressed or otherwise touched. But even this was viewed as cute: a sort of babyish coyness.

Until, that is, he reaches the age of five and our little Dimitris still hasn't spoken a single word. And in the meantime, his idiosyncrasies have gotten out of hand: if you so much as get close to him – let alone try and touch him – he starts kicking and screaming like a little devil. In all probability, the poor kid suffered from some form of autism. However, back then a condition like this was very hard to diagnose, and my parents didn't want the stigma that their firstborn had any defect.

So my mother will ship Dimitris off to Switzerland, to a mental hospital for children, where she herself will never once step foot, claiming that she 'can't bear the anguish' and has 'the other children to think of'. Only my father Minas goes there and back every now and then, taking time off work which is as important to him as life itself, in order to see his son, his baby, growing up like a dumb animal. A little after his fortieth birthday, after one such heartrending visit, he'll suffer a mild stroke which will leave a permanent paralysis on the left half of his face.

Relatives, neighbours and miscellaneous busybodies are told that, at the age of two, Dimitris contracted a rare case of encephalitis which left him brain-damaged for good.

Besides, there were more children to come.

More sickness to hide.

His Eyes

If one thing had indelibly smeared the soul of the adolescent Irini as she saw the world around her crumble and vanish, it was the loss of beauty: their handsome two-storey house in Samsun, her luxurious clothes, the euphony of the French language, the songs she used to sing at the Conservatory. During her entire life, she would struggle to find that long-lost exquisiteness once again – and life would go against her wishes in every possible way.

The year is 1939. In a short while, Greece is going to be swallowed up by the war, yet my father won't serve in the army. Initially his brass-hat brother will declare him *father of an invalid child* and then the stroke he suffered will render him unfit once and for all. In the autumn, Myron emerges from the womb; the second-born, whom, however, my mother shall always view as her firstborn: the first one that came out right – that's how she pictures him as she strokes her distended belly.

However, bad luck won't give the poor woman a break. Myron is born with a full head of thick black hair, and a case of strabismus just as striking. In vain does the doctor try to assure her that this flaw may correct itself over time. The months pass and reality is dishearteningly plain: Myron is cross-eyed.

For the first time, Papa Minas is furious with his beloved. "Two children you gave me, and they're both freaks. It's as if I married into the circus!"

Mama Rini wails and sobs. "He's your *son,* what does it matter if he squints a bit?"

"A *bit?* He can look at his breakfast with one eye and his dinner with the other!"

And so on and so forth. Stubbornly, my mother refuses to accept that this unfortunate finishing touch spoils indeed the picture of baby perfection that little Myron is. She fattens him up like a prize pig (it'll take him many long, hard years to drop his childhood flab), and shows him off to her woman friends as Nature's most sublime creation. Even when her third son, Kostakis, lays dying and wheezing in the crib, stricken by a bad case of whooping cough contracted from his older brother Myron, her sole concern is not the moribund infant but her treasured firstborn, who's coughing his poor heart out. Kostakis is buried unmourned.

Half a century later, a few days after Rini's death, a neighbourhood priest from the island of Tinos will track me down to inform me that for fifty years in a row, never missing one, Mrs Horianos gave him a votive offering to take to the famous icon of the miracle-working Virgin Mary: a pair of big, beautiful eyes etched on a piece of silver.

"For his eyes, Father," she'd say. "For my baby's poor eyes." Even though Myron was forty at the time and a father of two himself.

By the Pricking of My Thumbs...

...something wicked this way comes.
For most of the family and the world at large, wickedness will be incarnated in the form of my older sister Cleo. I, too, shall believe it.

But now I know. The evil approaching was me.

The Sinister Hand

In the spring of 1946, my brother Aegisthus is born. I wonder, did my mother know what an unfortunate name she'd given her own son? Luckily, someone must have told her something, because she shortened it to Agis.

Agis is born with a heart of gold. He will love me more than any other woman in his life and he'll be the man of my dreams. If you find the thought of siblings in love disturbing, you should have seen the two of us together...

But his birth isn't devoid of drama, either. Despite his blond locks and his cute little face, Agis's blue eyes are also crossed – imperceptibly so compared to Myron's, yet perfectly straight they are not. And since it will be necessary to wear thick-lensed glasses from the age of two (he's very short-sighted just like his brother), this slight imperfection will be magnified.

By now, Mama Rini is resigned to her fate: some women bear twins, some have stillborns, and she is destined to make squinters.

Even though he'll grow up under the shadow of our mother's favourite son, Myron, Agis will never hold a grudge against life like my sister Cleo will. He'll endure uncomplainingly the misfortunes that beset him: his lisping, the taunting and bullying of his older brother, his bad grades at school and his left-handedness which his mother will try and beat out of him. It will be Zoë who stops her when she gets too carried away with the thrashing of the poor child, though eventually Agis learns to write with his right hand, something which perhaps is responsible for his dyslexia. (And yet, decades later, I remember him playing football with his son Minas, and shooting – naturally – with his left foot. Human nature won't change, no matter how much violence it's subjected to).

Maybe my mother ought to have stopped at three (or, as she saw it herself, two) children. But my father was always chasing her around to 'mount' her, even in their old age, and apparently they hadn't gotten wind of condoms.

So, in The Year of Our Lord 1948, Cleo is born.

Banana Liqueur

Around the age of four, little Cleo, a chubby, naughty and gluttonous toddler, is left unsupervised for a few minutes, so she sneaks into the kitchen to rummage for some hidden treat – and deep in the cupboard under the sink she finds a bottle of banana liqueur. She's too young to read, but on the label there's the picture of a banana, and Cleo loves bananas more than anything in the whole wide world, therefore the yellowish liquid seems to her wildly desirable.

As luck has it, the bottle cap is a bit loose and she manages to unscrew it. She's already raised the bottle to her eagerly parted lips when Zoë comes into the kitchen, sees her, lets out a piercing shriek and wrenches the bottle from her stubby little hands – because the bottle doesn't contain banana liqueur but drain cleaner.

I'll be told this story a few years later, when I'll be already at the mercy of the tyrannical regime imposed by Myron and Cleo, who, envious of my special bond with Agis, submit us to daily torments.

And I'll keep fantasizing about a delightfully different ending to that story: Zoë walking into the kitchen too late, and my older sister thrashing and groaning on the floor, while the corrosive acid eats up her insides and she's drowning in her own blood.

Oh, we really loved each other to death, the Horianos siblings.

But Why?

Many times I will wonder about my older sister's inexorable pull towards destruction – her own, and the destruction of those close to her who made the mistake of treating her with love. I still wonder furtively, through my son, and have yet to find an answer.

I don't believe 'bad people' exist, even though I've been repeatedly burnt by actions which would appear like the definition of evil to any outsider. I don't think Cleo meant the damage she inflicted. Maybe she was urged by some undiagnosed pathology; or maybe it was her way of self-defence, a mistaken self-defence – as mistaken as every human thing is most of the time.

One thing is certain: during the first years of her life, when she most needed it, Cleo was deprived of love like one starved of food.

A Child Disowned

Let us re-examine the human backdrop of the Horianos family between the late 1940s and the early 1950s.

For starters, there is no visible father: he's been swallowed up by the store.

Mother is invisible, too. When not out shopping, spending her limitless pocket money on antiques, fancy wigs, and pastel-coloured suits, she's travelling with her husband under the pretext of importing luxury goods for the store, while her true purpose is the elevation, social and emotional, afforded by her jaunts abroad. (Papa Minas' view on travelling, aphoristic like the majority of his views, is: "Trees here, trees there. Houses here, houses there: what's the bloody difference?") At home Rini can be found only during stints of redecoration, where once again she ignores the animate décor (her four children, whom she has fully surrendered to the care of Zoë) in favour of new wallpapers, porcelain monstrosities, Oriental rugs and paintings: that is, with everything and anything that can keep her as far away as possible from the never-forgotten ghost of the shack in the slums.

Zoë is then nearly twenty and, despite her heart of gold, has her own shortcomings, the greatest and most dramatic of which is the uneven distribution of her love: she showers Agis and me with it, while only a few drops fall occasionally on Myron and Cleo.

And as for the four young siblings…

Myron, on the threshold of puberty, fat, cross-eyed and forever Mum's pet. First of his class at the German School, relentless nemesis of his brother Agis (whom he calls a 'dumbass' for his mediocre grades, and 'pussy' because of his weakness and inability to react aggressively to the various psychological forms of torture he subjects him to), and unholy ally of Cleo's, whom he also scorns but finds useful in the ploys he devises in order to disturb the peace and make his younger siblings suffer. (Sometimes I think that, after all is said and done, Myron might have been the sickest of us all…)

Agis finds himself in a constant state of confusion and panic, with Zoë as his sole protector, although the poor girl always has her hands full since she also takes care of the housework.

Cleo, the little devil – officially, too: Zoë calls her 'Lucifer'. Her only contact with her parents is the slaps and thrashings she receives for her numerous transgressions.

Last and least, me. The accident.

Accident in Milan

July 1952. To celebrate their wedding anniversary, Mr and Mrs Horianos travel to Milan – after much nagging by the alluring Rini (whenever it came to extracting money, my late mother could play the sex kitten with great success), who craves to milk her dearest Minas for all he's worth, and attacks his check book in the Galleria Vittorio Emanuele like the hawk plucks the hen.

And at night, in their suite at the Grand Hotel, Mama Rini gives herself to her husband with much insouciance and abandon, certain that, being by now over forty and having a womb repeatedly battered, she is unable to conceive anymore. If only.

(In fact, as if by instinct, the next morning she buys a wooden, bas-relief Madonna with Child – a young, pretty woman cradling a rosy-cheeked, sexless Jesus in her arms – although her home is otherwise entirely devoid of religious objects. I shall grow extremely fond of this particular Madonna and eventually hang her above my marital bed, despite my husband's intense dislike of what he sees as an intrusive piece of Catholic kitsch. Now it's been passed on to my own son, but his own husband, who actually has the same name as mine, won't let him show it off – and good for him: the gaudy Virgin has brought enough bad luck as it is).

How romantic and luxurious all this sounds, right? Conception in Milan, though not immaculate, under the canopy of such a wide bed that unwilling bodies need not touch… I'll fantasize about that magical evening many times, pondering on the first moment of my existence, although as my life and illness turned out, I never got to see Milan up close.

You see, Mum had recounted the entire story to me – and without omitting the key factor: that she neither wanted nor believed that she could become pregnant again.

A random, accidental existence: like slipping and falling; like taking a handful of pills hoping to finally sleep and dying instead.

Melek

My melek. That will be my mother's pet name for me. My angel. Even Dad, who, in his mid-fifties, half-paralyzed and with his hair completely white, looks more like my grandfather, moved perhaps by the fact that I've gotten both the name and the looks of his Vlach mother, grants me a rare term of endearment: *the little lamb*.

I'm a good-natured *agneau carnivore:* I eat whatever's on my plate. I go to bed without fussing, I accept bath-time or examined by the doctor forbearingly, smilingly.

It's not strange, of course; just sad that these three or four years of Heaven couldn't last a little longer.

I'm still too young and my parents' defenceless pet, so I'm not subjected to the daily hell meted out by the Myron-Cleo unholy alliance – but not so young that I don't comprehend deep in my soul the love that pours out of Zoë's and seven-year-old Agis's hearts like so much golden rain. If I was able to give love in years to come, it was because I gorged on it in my early life.

I grew up, however. And the angel turned into a demon.

I nearly forgot to say. I was born on April 2, 1953.

It was Holy Thursday.

Domestic Crimes

When four siblings out of four end up on medication by the age of forty, something very bad must have happened during their childhood.

Doctors tried to explain, to heal, at times even to conceal; spouses, affectionate and weary, struggled to cure with love, devotion, threats and indignation what couldn't – or wouldn't – be cured; and children were injured, some of them badly, while wading in the psychic minefield of people unfit to be parents.

Through these written lines, I'm still trying to understand. To look into the souls of those responsible, who were none others than those who raised us.

My parents, then: a rather crude father, prone to cruelty and sarcasm against those he considers his inferiors or minions, full of profound complexes and a nasty temper; when, at the age of seventy-eight, he'll show his sweet side for the first time, at the birth of my son, the entire family will be aghast – even I will think first of senility and then love. As to his own children, no sweetness is ever forthcoming: competitive with the boys, an ogre to the girls: one of those fathers who demanded to be called 'Sir' just by the sheer, rocky steepness of their physical presence.

My mother: a woman who has suffered adversity and humiliation, who has lived and grown old without knowing the pleasure of romantic love, and strives, like the heroine of a cheap sentimental novel, to fill her inner void with a load of the overpriced crap that the antique dealers and decorators of Thessaloniki keep plying her with. She takes frequent trips on her own and longs to move to Athens where she believes she'll be able to rub elbows with the heirs of old-monied, respectable aristocracy, but her husband refuses to give up his small-town prominence for big-town anonymity. And there are also the kids to consider...

And Zoë. A woman of good intentions yet deeply traumatized, with countless phobias (of dogs, cars, invisible dangers) which she will pass on as neuroses to the distant cousins she raises on her own, ignored by their parents and at the mercy of God, playing favourites with us in very clear and distinct ways, Stalinist almost: two of the children are treasures, and the other two are shit.

And then, in 1953, I enter the picture, breaking the proverbial camel's back for Mama Rini, who was looking for any excuse to avoid the burden of motherhood.

Her three older children (Myron, fourteen, Agis, seven, and Cleo, a mere five, poor thing, squealing and wailing: "I don't want to go to thchool!") become half-boarders at a private school: that is, they stay there after the lessons end until seven or eight in the evening when fed, exhausted and ready for bed (bunks in the same room, for God's sake, in a 2,000 square feet apartment) they return by taxi to a home which has become the vast playroom of little Katerina.

The reaction to this maternal act of treason – which even in my nonexistence I find vile and unforgivable – varies from sibling to sibling. Myron and Cleo view it as a challenge and vow to make my life miserable, whereas Agis, who is spared the taunting of Myron, is overjoyed and adores me even more.

But why would my useless mother do such a thing? What was it that bothered her so? Didn't she have her sanctum sanctorum with a four-poster bed always kept under lock and key – in order to partly escape the nocturnal humping – and even her own palatial bathroom, out of bounds to the rest of us who made do with a tiny cubby-hole and a bathtub slightly bigger than the inside of a coffin?

It defies explanation.

Anyway, it reminds me of a quote by Hitchcock, whom my son idolizes, used in the trailer for *Alfred Hitchcock Presents*:

It's time we brought murder back where it belongs: at home.

It Was the Best of Times

Do not think, though, that only tragedies befell the Horianos family and its luckless spawn. We also had a few great memories.

First and foremost, no matter how clichéd the phrase '*we wanted for nothing*' may sound, in our case it was true to the point of excess.

Was it a car Mama Rini's heart desired, so she could go on excursions to the popular seaside spots of Peraia and Baxe-Tsiflik without taking the bus with the hoi-polloi? Then her Minas would go out and get a car, one of the first to appear on the streets of Thessaloniki (this is 1931 we're talking about), a monstrously huge Ford imported straight from America, although he couldn't drive and never really learned to: I always remember him parking the beast with the front in first, and if Myron happened to make fun of him by pointing out that Dad didn't know how to reverse, Minas would grunt, "You son of a goat, I'm going forwards, what's the point of reverse? Why should I go backwards like some kind of crab?" And there were trips aplenty, whenever Mama Rini wanted to, or when we kids kept pestering her. We'd climb into the huge back seat and finally poor Zoë would squeeze in last, with half her bum squished against the window so as not to crowd us, while in the front seat Dad would be chain-smoking and Mum would tell him not to go so fast and he would reply that if she wanted a slow, leisurely ride he'd rent her a carriage with a dying horse so it could take a full two days to go to Epanomi Beach and back.

It was during one of these rides that Agis gave Dad the nickname *Hog-Slayer*.

We had just passed the outskirts of Phinicas – still an expanse of muddy fields back then, before the construction fever struck – when an enormous pig wanders into the road we're speeding down.

"For God's sake, Minas, hit the brakes," Mum orders.

But he just honks the horn without changing lanes.

Whereupon there's a massive thud as we drive right into the pig – we're talking serious car bodywork back then; today most cars would have been wrecked and the beast wouldn't have felt a thing – and we kids turn around and see the unfortunate beast on its back, trotters in the air.

"Oh no, Dad, you killed the poor little piggy," Cleo says, though judging by the way she was looking at it, she seemed sorrier that we couldn't roast it on a spit.

"Minas the Hog-Slayer," Agis says. "May this crime weigh on your soul."

And Dad retorts infuriated: "How was this *my* fault, you stupid boy? I kept honking and honking – the damn pig was deaf!"

During another outing to Peraia, there was a mishap which, though amusing in retrospect, might have ended in tears.

We're on this creaky wooden pier – I may not even have been born yet, but death's funny that way, it makes you think as if you've lived since the dawn of time – and suddenly one of the rotten planks gives in and Agis, still a toddler (which means I definitely don't exist), tumbles through the gap and into the sea.

Not that it was that deep – two feet at most – but suddenly the rest of the gang just look at one another in bafflement and horror: my parents can't swim, Myron is chasing after Cleo who's jealous and wants to dive in as well, so who's left to save Agis? Dear Zoë, unable to swim either, but just like the adoptive mother in Brecht's *Caucasian Chalk Circle* feared nothing at that moment.

So the blessed woman jumps into the sea, grabs Agis and raises him out of the water while she stands on the sandy bottom and, with her own head underwater, starts to drown.

Luckily, a man walking near the shore at that moment, sent probably by God, had heard all the ruckus, rushed into the water and retrieved both Agis – who was absolutely fine – and Zoë, blue-faced and half-dead, who retched half the Thermaikos Gulf before regaining her senses.

(Is it any wonder, then, that in moments of great sorrow, all the Horianos kids – or the Country Bumpkins, as our classmates called us because our Dad was old and coarse while our Mum dressed up like Jackie Kennedy in pastel suits with matching hats, purses and high heels – would rush into Zoë's comforting arms and whisper, '*You're our real Mum*'?)

Also, because Mama Rini demanded it, like all self-respecting plutocrats – never mind that our money was so new it was still hot off the press – we used to rent a cottage in the picturesque village of Platamon, where we'd frolic in the snow in the winter and enjoy the sea during the summer.

We'd even go there off-season; whenever Mum was visited by the Spirit of Urgent Redecoration, we were sent off packing to Platamon along with Dad and Zoë, so she could go nuts with the furniture people and the various decorators her obedient husband paid through the nose for.

As for us kids, the Pactolus River flowed steadily. School, foreign language tutors, music classes, ballet lessons, sports – you name it. Pocket money whenever we asked for it and for whatever we wanted to splurge it on – cigarettes, books and records for me, clothes and imported cosmetics for Cleo, and for our brothers, fistfuls of money to throw around and impress the It-girls of that day and age – treating everyone in the patisserie to ice cream and soft drinks, posing as the eligible bachelors they imagined themselves to be.

And the food, oh God, the food we consumed in that house! It's no mystery that Myron and Cleo ended up like blimps before they even hit puberty – what's really amazing is the fact that Agis and I managed to remain skinny.

Say we had a hankering for chestnuts – but not just chestnuts. Myron would want a chestnut cake, Agis some boiled, chocolate-covered chestnuts, Cleo a box of *marrons glacés* and I a bag of roasted ones, not roasted on the kitchen stove though but from a street vendor. Meaning that Zoë had to run like Daffy Duck back and forth all over the city to accommodate everybody's tastes and Papa Horianos spent insane amounts of money until we'd had our fix.

There's a forest of chestnut trees on Mount Hortiatis, towering over Thessaloniki. Well, come autumn, we'd pick those bastards clean.

It's not a small thing to grow up without ever being deprived of a single thing – it's a huge deal, actually, even if we took it too far and ended up dumb as bricks because of all this pampering. It's really something owning a first edition of *Bonjour Tristesse*, delivered days after it had hit the shelves in France, or a signed Beatles album.

Yet, for some reason, despite the Amalthean splendour of our home, it was its underlying poisonous sickness that stayed with us. In years to come, therefore, those luxuries would seem insignificant and pointless.

In a book I read through my son (this is one of the great things about having been loved: you get to read books even after you're gone), two sisters, raised with a silver spoon like us, are talking.

'*Thank God for simple pleasures*', says the older sister to the younger one.

And the younger replies, '*But why do they have to be so simple?*'

The Photo

"Smile, Katerinaki" – little Katherine – "Say 'cheese'!"
And I do.

Why does Myron torture us with such malevolence, why does he take pleasure in our anguish? Perhaps, being Mum's firstborn, her pet, he's had time to develop the only child's brattiness and views us as intruders: in his room, in the heart of Mama Rini, in his unclouded existence. I hesitate to call it sadism, because I do not know if he suffered from a disorder, poor kid, or if he simply inflicted violence upon us knowing he was the stronger.

Whatever the cause, over the years Myron turned into our worst nightmare. Agis, the second-born son, the bad student with the skinny fragile frame, is the butt of his pitiless jibes and cruel jokes: *sissy, squirt* and *retard* are the mildest epithets he uses, until my poor brother – seven years younger than Myron – runs sobbing into Zoë's reassuring embrace – which feeds Myron's hate even more. With Cleo, things are even simpler, if more savage: she's a lard-arse, a beached whale, a pregnant cow, lucky not to live in a village where they'd slaughter and roast her fatty rump – a taunting that makes little Cleo, nine years Myron's junior, react either with outbursts of fury, or with fits of crippling despair and insecurity: she's too ashamed of her weight to go to school, or for a walk, terrified that everyone will be watching her with the same disgust as her older brother: *Here comes Piggy*.

And what about Little Katerina? Ah, the runt of the litter is already a scaredy-cat because she's so little and also infinitely gullible. So Myron keeps devising ways to terrorize me. Seeing how much Zoë loves me, he takes me aside and explains very seriously that the reason she has such love for me is that I'm her actual daughter, albeit of an unknown father, which means I'm a bastard, and that the people who consent to treat me as their daughter could toss both of us out in the street any day now.

Not that it takes such intricate fabrications to scare me. Take the Lair of the Poo Witch, for instance: soon after I turn three and learn to use the little W.C. everyone shares except our prissy mother, Myron convinces me that in the storeroom between our bedroom and the toilet lives a demon named the Poo Witch, who goes out at night to hunt children down and drink their blood. And every night he keeps plying me with sour cherry juice, so I'll get up in the dead of the night desperate to pee and he will sit on his top bunk and watch me shaking like a leaf in the dimness of the corridor, terrified that the moment I take another step, the Poo Witch will open the door of the storeroom and pounce onto me. Often I'm so paralyzed with fear, I don't make it to the toilet and wet myself, and if Zoë doesn't wake up to change me and my wailing disturbs our mother's sleep, I also get a spanking for scaring her in the black of night.

My biggest fear, however, is heights. Even though we live in a first-floor apartment, I never dare go out on the balcony – I take only a couple of tiny steps, provided there's someone standing in front of me, blocking the view that makes me faint with terror. I even start crying when I'm made to sit on a stool that's too tall, like a kitten that's climbed so high it can't get back down on its own.

Myron, of course, has exploited my phobia to the limit: during a family outing to the café located at the top of the White Tower, while everybody's busy with their ice cream sundaes, he grabs me and holds me right on the ledge, telling me, "Look at the lovely view, Katerinaki!" And naturally I start squealing and Dad slaps Myron across the face and Mum gives me a slap on the bum as well, because – she's done it again, the cursed brat! – I've wet my panties, certain that Myron was going to drop me.

And yet I still trust my oldest brother completely. Like a beaten dog, I never hold a grudge, and a single kind word or gentle caress makes me forget all the torments he's submitted me to.

So here we are on that fateful day.

Myron has just got a brand-new camera as a birthday present and he's been taking pictures of me nonstop, laughing at the way I make eyes saying 'cheese'. So, when he suggests putting me on top of the wardrobe in Dad's bedroom so I'll look like a statue on its pedestal, I'm fooled fright away, even though my heart shakes at the sight of the seven-foot wardrobe, which, to someone as tiny as I am, looks about as tall as an apartment building.

Next thing I know, I'm up there – so high up I've started unawares to whimper. But Myron, speaking in a velvety, soothing voice, convinces me once more that I'm in no danger, no danger at all, don't be silly, even if you slip and fall I'll catch you, don't you trust your own brother? Of course I do – I'm four and he is seventeen. So I regain my courage bit by bit and start posing again, tittering and shrieking at the jokes Myron makes to make me forget my fear.

Then, suddenly: "Now wait a second," he says. "I'll just go to my room and develop the photos, so you can see how pretty you look."

And Little Katerina waits and waits, until the smile trembles and fades from her lips. And then comes terror, wild and powerful like a monster, and I start crying and screaming, but Myron has closed the bedroom door behind him, and by sheer bad luck the house is deserted – even Zoë, usually close to the rescue, is on the roof with our washerwoman, Simela, helping her hang the Horianos family's endless laundry out to dry.

Mama Rini will be the one to find me – hours later, face drenched with tears, voice hoarse from howling, my corduroy dungarees soaked in pee – and take me down from the wardrobe.

She won't give Myron a beating, he's too old for that and besides she could never bear to strike him, but she'll do something even worse. "That's why God made you cross-eyed," she'll tell him. "So your eyes match the ugliness of your soul."

Smile, Little Katerina.

The Murdered Tutu

When her daughter turns five, Mama Rini decrees that Katerina, as befits any young girl of good stock, should take ballet lessons post-haste.

And, lavish as ever, she presents me with a complete ballerina's costume, removing it from an enormous white box like a wedding dress: white leotard, eggshell satin slippers, and a resplendent tutu, plump and fluffy like a cloud and softer than a breeze to the touch.

As is to be expected of a girl my age, I am so thrilled by my new outfit, I demand to try it on at once, promising that I won't even eat if Mum doesn't let me wear it till bedtime.

However, lurking in the shadowy corners of our home into which I roam giggling and performing clumsy pirouettes is Cleo who – understandably; she's a ten-year-old girl – feels so furious she's about to explode.

So she goes and finds Mum and declares that she, too, wants to take ballet lessons, and wants a tutu just like mine, only better.

"You're not ballet material, dear," the tender-hearted mother replies. "You're already tall, you walk all crookedly – plus you're too fat to be a ballerina."

Which not only makes Cleo (who, despite the blows, both literal and figurative, of all these years, remains a little girl) hate her own graceless and overweight self, but her puny, bony sister even more.

Thus when night falls and after I've taken off my outfit under penalty of getting the belt, and hung it up in a prominent spot inside the wardrobe, Cleo, sleepless and restless, climbs off her bunk cradling the tailoring scissors she's pilfered from Zoë's knitting basket and cuts the tutu to ribbons.

Next morning, upon wakening, I see my ravaged tutu and start screaming. Zoë rushes over, but my desolate wails have already awoken Mum who forces a confession from Cleo with a couple of backhand slaps. "Damn you, you vile creature!" she cries, and goes on slapping her, sending the occasional slap in my direction as well in hope of shushing me up.

Whereupon Papa Horianos invades the scene of the early-morning drama, tall and stout and furious – a fearsome figure. "What devil has possessed you at the crack of dawn, you bloody wenches?" he demands and I try to explain what happened, sobbing all the time, and Cleo is also crying, and Mum has collapsed into a chair because she only has one lung left and she's worn it out with all the beating, and finally Dad starts yelling with his booming ogre's voice, scaring us shitless and effectively shutting us up.

"You, slut, I should send you to work in a cathouse!" he bellows at Cleo (I'll only learn the true meaning of the word – not a house full of cats, at any rate – years later from Agis, who hadn't missed a second of the incident). "But you're lucky it's Sunday. So, if I pay for both of you to become ballerinas, will you make peace and shut your holes, or shall I fetch my belt and skin you alive?"

And on the afternoon of the very next day we are given two brand-new tutus, identical bar their sizes. However, I never went to a single ballet lesson. My childish heart was heavy with the memory of my first tutu which Cleo, in her meanness, had murdered with a pair of scissors.

The Horrors of Others: The Extended Family

But let us take a look at the rest of the clan.

Firstly, our mother's sisters: Aunt Ariadne and Aunt Fotini.

The former, a woman of exquisite beauty, married a textile factory owner from Thessaloniki – but her disorder has already shown its first symptoms. A little after their honeymoon cruise around the Mediterranean, she comes to our place and confides to her older sister that Vlassis, her husband of a few weeks, on the night of their nuptials and every night that followed, has been raping her – in fact, sodomizing her. Mama Rini nearly has a stroke, so she calls Vlassis at once, and the poor man breaks into tears of relief, because, according to his version of the events, Ariadne had disembarked the cruise ship at Rhodes, after stealing some money from his wallet while he slept, and had been missing for ten whole days – which he spent searching for her frantically all over the Aegean Sea. And when Mum, who was suspicious to begin with, corners her sister, Ariadne confesses that she ran away.

"And what on earth did you do in Rhodes, you bloody fool, a woman all alone in a strange place?"

"I fucked sailors," is Ariadne's coquettish reply.

The shock is so great that even though they're grown women, our mother slaps her sister across the face.

To make a long story short, Vlassis comes running to our place along with Dad and a psychiatrist, who has a brief consultation with Ariadne, sedates her and says he would like to have her committed to a mental hospital the better to diagnose her condition, were it not for the fact that Ariadne, as he had determined during his examination, was several months pregnant – so advanced, in fact, that it was doubtful whether

Vlassis was actually the father. However, our uncle had a heart of gold; not only he didn't begrudge his wife the possible premarital cuckolding and its consequences, but held her in his arms as if she was a wounded little bird and vowed that he'd help her get well and that the child, in his eyes, was his and his alone, end of story.

Thus is born my cousin Eva, who in years to come will be my closest, most beloved friend. But as divine retribution for her mother's sin – at least that's how Ariadne views it, sobbing on her sister's bosom some months later – Eva is born with a large birthmark on her cheek, which requires special treatment abroad in order to be removed. "I don't want her, Rini dear," our aunt wails. "That monster is no child of mine. It's Satan's offspring, he raped me in the arse each night on the boat." The daughter flies off with her father to Switzerland and her mother is hospitalized for a round of electroconvulsive therapy.

As a result of the radiation treatment at so young an age (at least that's what the doctors ascribed it to back then), Eva will exhibit a precocious growth rate. At the age of eight she will get her first period, and by ten she'll develop big, round breasts; at twelve, she'll look as tall and fully grown as any adult female, so much so that she'll start getting in to cinemas to watch NC-17 films.

Ariadne will never truly love her daughter. She'll never forgive Eva the fact that, whereas she had been gorgeous, the fruit of her loins is a rather plain girl. The first time she'll come upon her half-naked in her room, studying in puzzlement her newly blossomed breasts in the mirror, she'll tell her scornfully: "If you ever find yourself a man, just make sure to turn all the lights off before you undress." Poor Eva succumbs to a violent depression and spends six whole months in bed, refusing to go to school or even feed herself, so her mother sends her off again to Switzerland, this time to be hospitalized in a psychiatric clinic for teenagers.

Despite the years she'll spend abroad, studying and managing over time to make a normal, satisfying life for herself, Eva will carry around her mother's illness like a cross she has to bear. Her father's early death will bring her unwillingly back to Greece and Ariadne – who, in spite of numerous stints in mental hospitals and all the pills she's taking, will continue sneaking out of the house and sexually assaulting unknown men in the streets (once, after an absence of an entire month, she is found working in a whorehouse like one of the regular girls). Living with Ariadne will wreck Eva.

Honour thy father and thy mother – and see where that gets you.

Then there's Mum's youngest sister, Fotini, or Auntie Fifi, as we all call her – everyone but Dad, the most foul-mouthed man I met in my whole life (with the possible exception of my son), who usually refers to her as '*your shit-for-brains sister*'.

Even though she's not the sharpest knife in the drawer (Myron's milder assessment), Auntie Fifi manages just fine: at thirty, an old maid by the standards of that day and age, she meets Gus, a middle-aged man with a Greek restaurant in Astoria, New York, who is recently widowed and childless and on the lookout for a woman to take care of him.

Fotini devotes herself to him completely, and although she's unable to conceive, the two of them will have the happiest of marriages and live to a ripe old age together (even as an eighty-year-old widow, Auntie Fifi will burst to tears at any mention of Gus). They will adopt a young girl from a town near Larissa and raise her lovingly, doting on her: my cousin Kostoula, owner and manager of her father's restaurant to this day and mother of eight, if you please.

So why have I included Fotini in this chapter?

The reason was a photo, sent from New York along with the misspelled and slightly pious letters Auntie Fifi regularly wrote to her oldest sister.

For a few months after her wedding and expatriation, the sweet, naïve Fotini is convinced by a devious woman married to a dentist that a pair of dentures is not just the natural outcome for every human being, but actually much preferable to our natural teeth – and so Auntie Fifi goes and has thirty-two healthy teeth extracted.

And as if that weren't bad enough, she goes to a photo booth and takes a snapshot, proudly holding up her brand-new sparkling dentures, while her wide, broad grin reveals her still bloody gums.

Lastly, a few words about my father's family.

Of the eight children of father Dimitrós Horianos, the three girls will all die before their twenties: the first two of fever and the last one of tuberculosis. Panos, the youngest sibling, joins the guerrilla army after the end of WWII and is killed in an ambush set up under the orders of his older brother, a high-ranking officer of the national militia. He's only twenty-five.

As to our Uncle Vangos the Commie-Slayer, fate has in store a severe retribution for his fratricidal crimes: his twin daughters, Elsa and Dora, at the age of seven, fall into a dried-up well hidden in the undergrowth and are killed, while he spends the last decade of his life in a vegetative state as a result of a massive stroke (or of syphilis, according to my father, who'd never stopped hating his brother).

I learn all these details from Agis in my teens; also that the 'Gang War', as many of our school teachers referred to it, was in fact an actual civil war, complete with heroes and scoundrels.

Therefore, in my simple mind, the story of our uncle and his daughters takes the perspective of an ancient Greek tragedy with the requisite catharsis. You'd be right, of course, to think, *Wait, he might have been a monster — but how was that the poor little girls' fault?*

Well, it wasn't. No one's guilty, or we all are. Or both.

Be that as it may, those two young cousins who never got to grow up, to live, who departed this world while in the midst of innocence and joy, will be the object of my envy many times in years to come. A furious, white-hot envy.

The Quiet Years

It's such a pity that I remember so little of what happened between my fifth and twelfth birthdays — although, thankfully, those weren't the only blissful years of my life.

All that remain are a few scattered images and feelings.

It's during those years that I become fluent in French, taking vengeance on Cleo who is terrible at learning foreign languages and would rather have her eyes gouged out with a red-hot poker than read a book.

It's during those years that my beloved brother Agis, an adolescent of thirteen with the tastes and sensibilities of a much older man, teaches me about books and music without pressuring or patronizing me: he simply shares with me all that he loves passionately, letting me find my way towards my own profound passions. For instance, although he's a fervent fan of Mikis Theodorakis (and goes recklessly to clandestine record-playing gatherings at friends' homes, or shuts himself in our room to listen through headphones so Mama Rini won't freak out with the 'Commie songs'), I become a lifelong devotee of

Manos Hadjidakis, whose passing, thirty-five years later, I'll mourn more than the death of my own father.

It's during those years that I become aware of the fact that, as if to spite my obese and envious sister and also our mother who's not big on compliments that aren't directed at her firstborn, I am beautiful, so beautiful that I catch the eye of people when they first meet me, like a wildflower incongruously blossoming in the midst of a Rococo nightmare.

It's during those years that I decide when I grow up I'm going to marry a man just like Agis and have only one kid, so he or she won't have to share my love with a sibling. I'm still too young to imagine myself as a mother, but I aspire to become a slightly more well-read version of Zoë, whom I love and snub at the same time, just like all children with their parents. Perhaps, without being aware of it, through my sisterly love and devotion, I end up making Agis way too demanding of the girlfriends he meets on the sly after school – although I've never believed that too much love can hurt you.

Those pleasurable and quiet years we owe to the fact that Myron is studying philosophy at the Sorbonne – so we live free of his tyranny and the unbearable shadow he used to cast upon our lives. Each night, our mother locks herself in her boudoir and cries inconsolably; and the next day, almost every single day, she sticks packs of bank-smooth, colourful franc notes between the pages of thick leather-bound books and sends them to her precious boy who's living it up in Paris, screwing around like his life depends on it.

Years as radiant as a lie, as the midnight sun.

To be followed by an equally radiant darkness.

The First Attack

The seat of the old bus that's taking us to the French-speaking high school I attend has a small rip across its leather surface. Every morning, as soon as I sit down, I thrust my hand beneath my school uniform skirt and stick my finger into the rip, pulling it as if it's a scab on a wound. As the tear keeps getting bigger and wider day by day, in the same way something inside me is being torn as well: an unseen trauma.

Until, one winter morning, my mind is suddenly inundated by this image:

The bus is speeding ahead and I'm running down the aisle, I open the passenger door and leap out right into the wheels of the oncoming vehicles whose drivers have no time to hit the brakes, so I'm squashed like a mouse: gore and bone shards and blue uniform tatters and one bloody shoe lying in the asphalt.

I close my eyes to shut away this horrible scene, but it is persistent; in fact, more images flood the trembling darkness of my lids:

I'm opening the window and jumping out of the moving bus – I'm so thin I can easily squeeze through.

I'm pouncing on the driver, grabbing him by the neck and causing him to lose control, with the result that the bus rushes into the opposite lane and drives straight into a truck and all of us are turned into ground meat.

Or I simply go mad. I've no idea how it is to lose your mind, but never in my life have I feared anything more: the mere thought, the energetic verb *to go insane* is worse than death and *to die*, its black vortex more horrifying than nonexistence.

It is the first time this happens to me and I use every ounce of strength I have to stifle my terror, so that by the time we arrive at school I'm wiped out, as if I've just taken a beating by a pair of heavy, pitiless hands, and the tear on the bus seat spreads from one end of the cushion to the other, the leather ribbons drooping like flesh torn apart by a sword.

The next time, however, as soon as the images assail me, something inside me snaps and with a scream I faint.

I'm fetched back home in a hurry by Dad; he is so upset that he has forgotten all about the store which, without his ever-present leadership, may go under at any moment. The family doctor – a paediatrician – examines me and picks up just a slight tachycardia since I've calmed down considerably by then. He asks me if I've had my period yet, and I answer no, which is the truth (perhaps because of my extreme thinness, my period will not start until I've almost turned sixteen). As soon as the doctor leaves, my mother, distrustful by nature, orders me to show her my underwear in case I'm lying.

But what I've lost is much less simple than blood. Whether because of her sister Ariadne, or as a result of what little maternal instinct she possesses, Mama Rini eyes me suspiciously and swears me on my life to tell her exactly what happened, down to the last detail. And though part of me knows I must keep the truth hidden from everyone, even from Agis, I give in and blurt out the whole story.

My mother listens to me unperturbed, and when I finish she says: "These are the words of a diseased mind. Don't you ever breathe a single word about all this to anyone, you poor thing, because you'll end up in the loony bin." (In retrospect, I've laughed my heart out at this memory – at the accuracy of Mama Rini's prediction.)

"Okay, fine. But I'm not getting on a bus ever again," I reply.

"I don't give a damn. I'll get you a chauffeur. But keep your mouth shut. Not a word."

It's not as if I was planning to shout it from the rooftops.

It was thus that I met my own monster with its iron teeth; and by keeping its existence a secret, it was as if I was saying to it, *Don't leave.*

The Horrors of Others: Marianne

To the immense sorrow of his mother who intended to marry him to the daughter of an industry magnate – she'd already done half the matchmaking – after the end of his studies, Myron meets and falls in love with a girl one year his senior called Marianne, a middle-class Belgian beauty, who works as a piano teacher. That, at least, will somewhat console Mama Rini, who's already out looking to buy the grand piano that will blend perfectly with our drawing-room furniture; the piano that is to be played by her flawless grandchildren.

Indeed, Marianne returns to Greece with Myron, and on the day of their wedding, which takes place with great pomp at the Thessaloniki Cathedral, is already two months pregnant. As for her hubby, he is sadly labouring away, because Papa Minas has made himself clear: "Besides the house I bought not for your ugly mug but for my grandson, you won't see a dime from me. Either you start working at the store, or you roll your degree into a slingshot and go hunting for wild pigeons to eat. The choice is yours." So Myron ends up an employee instead of a philosopher, doing a job he despises, and is awful at it until he retires.

Marianne, the most elegant pregnant woman in recorded history, is always excessively polite toward us, but I sense that she harbours some undefined fear, stemming either from our family's tainted aura or, even more likely, from her cohabitation with Myron. Since she hasn't learned any Greek yet, she can converse only with Mum (who retains a bit of French from her youth) and me. Of course, my age and the blood I share with Myron stand in the way of her becoming a bosom buddy and thus being able to confide in me, however on one occasion, when we find ourselves all alone in our apartment, I ask her right out: "Do you love him?"

Oddly, Marianne startles me by answering in mispronounced yet accurate Greek: "Love eez a stoopid shing." Her reply will bother me for a long time: how can you call love *stupid?* And what does that mean for your loved ones?

The ultimate explanation will come to me and everyone else a year later, when one fine morning Marianne will take her two-month-old daughter Irène and spirit her away, back to her parents' place in Belgium. Mama Rini wails and gnashes her teeth in vain for her vanished granddaughter; Myron will do nothing to reclaim his daughter, whom he will only see again after Marianne's death, when Irène is thirty years old.

Admittedly I too was mad with my sister-in-law back then, thinking her actions inexcusable, inhuman. It will take me years to understand that, in all probability, it was the desperate measure of a mother who wants to protect her child from something evil. Something profoundly evil.

Virginia Woolf

The book is blue, clothbound. I don't recall the title, just the name of the author because it sounds so much like *wolf.*

The book is read absorbedly by Alexandra, a plump, bespectacled classmate of mine who, just like me, has no friends at school. Alexandra is bilingual – her mother is British.

I start talking to her. She seems surprised – when she raises her eyes from the page, she has a sleepwalker's startled stare – but, like all lonely people, she quickly becomes quite talkative.

I ask her about the book she's reading and Alexandra begins to recount an incomprehensible plot – and then she tells me about the authoress, the misspelled she-wolf: that she was mad, heard voices, and in the end couldn't take it anymore and killed herself by filling the pockets of her cardigan with stones and walking into a river.

I listen to her transfixed and terrified. Mad? Heard voices? And what were those voices saying?

Nobody knows; she was hallucinating, poor woman; she was schizophrenic.

The unfamiliar, unheard-of words slip into my mind and find a nest awaiting them. Madness, my greatest fear – the end of the world. The thought of hearing voices, telling you to fill your pockets with stones and jump into a river.

And this unknown, horrible word: *schizophrenic*.

Like something in your mind is being torn apart, like the old leather seat in the bus, pulled open by the invisible finger of lunacy.

For the first but unfortunately not the last time, I'll wonder: *What if I'm schizophrenic?*

Of course, the ground has been laid by more panic attacks, by more mute and unspoken terror.

I am fourteen. Nowadays I only get into a car if the driver promises that he won't drive any faster than twenty miles per hour and that he'll stay glued to the outer lane, so that even if the dark urge to open the door and leap out becomes irresistible, I won't get killed.

I've twice already gathered up all the sharp knives in the

house and thrown them in the bin, along with Dad's and Agis's shaving kits; the one who gets scolded is 'careless Zoë' who, having guessed that it was my doing, hastens to take responsibility for any such mishap.

I'm so afraid I might suddenly attack and obliterate myself that I go to extremes: terrified that I'm going to swallow every aspirin in the house, I take one in front of Mum, run to the kitchen, break and swallow a raw egg, and then rush back to the living room where I throw up on her big and outrageously expensive Persian carpet – managing to convince Mama Rini that I'm allergic to aspirin. From that day forward, aspirin is banned from our house.

However, despite my exaggerated precautions and constant vigilance, there are moments when panic ambushes and overwhelms me and I have to run into Agis's or Zoë's arms, so they can hold me tight and reassure me with sweet words and caresses that I'm not dying, that my heart is not going to stop beating any moment now; that it's just that my – to use the expression employed in my family for years to come – '*nerves are worn out*'.

Fortunately, both the potential snitches and tormentors are gone during this delicate phase: Myron lives in Paris and Cleo in her new home, part of her dowry – she's recently got married to a polytechnics student in Köln who is never going to graduate, fifteen years older than her and currently unsuccessful manager of a store Dad bought for him. Plus, she's seven months pregnant.

Moreover, Agis handles my attacks, phobias and suicidal obsessions with the finesse and understanding of one afflicted himself, since over the years he too has developed a serious case of obsessive-compulsive disorder – although back then neither of us is familiar with the term: he just has '*frazzled nerves*' from time to time.

In his case, the crises revolve around rituals which he must perform religiously so his world doesn't collapse.

At night, for instance, the curtains and shutters have to be hermetically shut, so no ray of light, natural or electrical, may sneak through in the morning; the same goes for the door to the room we share, whose casement gaps he stuffs with towels. Needing to be certain that the curtains won't move during the night, initially he tapes them to the window frame and finally he buys dark blue sheets of paper to completely seal the tall windows.

Agis is an overwrought young man, inclined to panic whenever he has a paper to turn in or an exam to prepare for: for these tasks he wears at all times a specific red woollen sweater, old and worn and full of holes, which Zoë launders in secret so Mum won't notice it and throw it away. Moreover, all of his papers and writing materials must be specifically arranged and aligned on top of his desk and the reading lamp has to be turned to a specific angle. This lamp is a terrible hassle: if the light bulb goes out, he becomes frantic, as if it were the last bulb on earth; when we go for a walk (in my case all the more rare, because I'm terrified I'll suddenly leap into the oncoming traffic), he returns home three or four times to make sure he's turned the lamp off.

Unlike his younger sister, who resorts to sleep with the craving and ease of a person who views reality as a threat and therefore longs for blackness and the absence of conscious thought, Agis sleeps badly. He often stays up or starts suddenly from his sleep because he can't remember something: the name of a small-time actor, the successor to Queen Victoria, or the title of a French song – and so he rouses me quite frequently in the middle of the night and I sit up on the quilt that I spread across the floor to sleep (bunks have become an impossibility) and obediently recite the required information – lyrics, dates and first names of statesmen.

(The fact that these everyday woes completely elude our do-nothing mother's attention is, I think, indicative of the disease suffusing our entire family: a bunch of people accustomed to hide from the truth whenever it becomes even slightly unpleasant).

And all this time, I keep obsessing over Virginia Woolf, the schizophrenic suicide who heard voices. I've looked up and managed to obtain her books from the best bookshops in town, but I'm afraid to read them, lest they somehow infect me. Because what would I do if I suddenly started hearing voices too, telling me to fill my pockets with stones (where would I even find stones in the city?) and jump into the Thermaikos Gulf? (Which wouldn't carry me off like a fast river, causing the shame to disappear along with my corpse, but stagnant as it is, would expose me to everyone: here floats Katerina the madwoman.)

In the peak of my despair, I've gone to a nearby church and confessed to a priest my greatest terror, the panic attacks, and also about the moments when it's as though something is urging me to harm myself. And this generally sweet-spoken and mild person is adamant: these thoughts are planted into my head by Satan, who is tempting me to commit the gravest sin of all, a sin punished by the refusal to be buried in consecrated ground, followed by an eternity in Hell. His suggestion? I should confess and take communion regularly and any time these thoughts besiege me, fall on my knees and repeat ten, twenty, a hundred times – as long as it takes to banish the evil within me – the phrase: *Lord Jesus Christ, Son of God, have mercy on me, the sinner*.

His advice won't work, no matter how fervently I beseech

Jesus to have mercy on me, the sinner; at the same time Hell, that sword of Damocles, will be added to my list of fears and over the years become the worst of them: not only the terror of death, but an eternal hellfire as well.

(Despite my nonexistence, the more I think about it, the more furious it makes me. I find nothing more obscene than the terrorizing of ordinary people with the arbitrarily defined invention that goes by the name of sin. Hell, huh? Well, come and spend one single day inside my mind – let alone a month or thirty years – and then tell me what Hell feels like.)

Luckily, other forms of human invention are helping me out.

First and foremost, music, my salvation; I fill my ears, mind and soul, listening to my favourite records with the volume cranked up, so that no other voice can sneak through.

Quizás, Quizás, Quizás. Aline. Que Sera, Sera. Fever. The 7-inch records are worn thin from being played over and over, while I sway in sweet deliverance.

And at nights when I can't listen to music, I read insatiably until my eyes grow heavy and the book falls from my hands; books that make me laugh so hard (*The Diary of a Nobody, Three Men In a Boat, Tristram Shandy, Oblomov,* PG Wodehouse and Edward Lear's *Nonsense Poems*) that sometimes I wake Agis up, while he is struggling to recall Disraeli's first name, and read excerpts to him, tittering at two in the morning.

And then, one autumn afternoon, Virginia Woolf comes back.

It's been over a year since I've been to the movies; the mere thought of the crowds unnerves me – never mind questions like what am I supposed to do if suddenly there's a fire or an earthquake? Or if I go mad while being in the cinema and start screaming?

But, as luck would have it, a movie theatre close by is playing *Who's Afraid of Virginia Woolf?* starring Elizabeth Taylor and Richard Burton. The film has an NC-17 rating, but with Agis – a twenty-year-old law student – accompanying me and a small bribe to one of the ushers we are free to watch whichever film we like.

Yet why should I choose a film with a title like that? I know nothing of the story, but to be inappropriate for younger audiences it probably has upsetting scenes: Virginia Woolf going insane or killing herself. Normally, in the same way I've avoided her books expressly, I should do the same with the film bearing her name. But the temptation is too great: to see at last the unknown face of schizophrenia, the mind torn apart, hoping or realizing that it looks nothing like mine, so that my haunting fear may subside.

I have no recollection whatsoever of either the cinema or the film itself: I only remember leaping from my seat at some point, overcome by a panic unlike anything I'd felt in my whole life, running out of the cinema – like a madwoman – and stumbling in front of a car, whose driver luckily managed to hit the brakes; it merely knocked me over onto the street, terrified and with a couple of bruises, but otherwise sound – physically, at least.

This time things had gone too far. Stigma or no stigma, this thing can't be put off any longer.

It is decided that I must see a doctor.

Undress, Katerinaki

We fear and obey our doctors; we respect and believe them; for their role is to rid us of disease.

Therefore, I eagerly surrender to the care of Dr G., a

neurologist, psychiatrist and professor at the Thessaloniki Medical School, in order to help me get rid of my fears and the panic attacks which may prove fatal.

Dr G. has a friendly, almost paternal, countenance – even though I'm not quite sure what that means: Papa is sixty-five now, an old man constantly absent. Nevertheless, I follow him to the examination room, and when he tells me to undress so he may perform the necessary auscultations and palpations, I have no reason to doubt him: I am in good hands, hands that cure and teach.

But instead of the stethoscope's cold bell, which I'm anticipating with the occasional shiver, I feel Dr G.'s bare fingers struggling with the buckle of my bra, undoing it, and then his right hand cupping my small breast, while he tells me to take a deep breath. I comply, but instead of exhaling I let out a piercing scream.

Stigma, trauma… how easily, how unthinkingly, we use these words.

I'll be fighting bipolar disorder for thirty-five years. A losing battle.

And that is because I'll never trust a shrink again. I only wish I was just as distrustful where pills were concerned.

And no, I don't like cursing others.

Castoff

I have discovered an interesting game.

When you spread out misery like the flu to whomever comes your way, it feels as if it grows smaller.

I don't know if that makes me a bad person.

But I've no wish to be good; only less miserable, if possible.

For instance.

I begin to smoke right in my parents' faces.

Oddly, my father's reaction is rather mild.

"I didn't make you pretty so that you blow smoke out of your nostrils like a dragon."

For my mother, however, when I light up in front of her and blow the smoke nonchalantly, I commit the most grievous sacrilege – tip my ash into a monstrous, gilt-encrusted ashtray intending solely for my mother's friends' admiring glances. She slaps me, grabs my hair and starts yelling:

"You filthy girl, have you no shame, smoking in front of your own mother?"

I shove her away so violently, she topples back onto the sofa and for a few moments remains supine like an upended turtle.

"Screw you and your fucking ashtrays," I say. "But that's why your kids ended up wrong in the head – because you love the trash you buy more than us."

Mama Rini, hair tussled, cheeks red, overall pathetic, stares at me wide-eyed, parting her lips and trembling; she is ready to say that I'm mad, that she should lock me up in an asylum – but then she remembers her oldest son withering away in a loony bin in Athens (no more posh clinics in Switzerland: Papa Minas has a bunch of kids to provide for). She rises and darts off to her boudoir, dissolving into sobs.

I sit up, retrieve the still-burning cigarette from the floor (it's actually left a black burn mark on the polished wood – what joy!) and go on pretending to be a cool, poised smoker, although I'm shaking on the inside, tormented by guilt and about to start crying myself for upsetting poor Mum.

But I resist the urge. For if I start crying, I may never stop.

Yet why am I unhappy?

I don't know. I only know that when I wake up in the morning, I wish I'd died in my sleep. And then I lie still as a corpse and stare at the ceiling, because I can't budge, the sheet weighs so much it might as well be made of metal, while the room, the house, my very life, they're all closing in on me. Stifling me.

I feel like a burden on earth, that's all I know. And I envy everyone else, the strangers in the street who seem so happy, even if they're unaware of their own happiness and look glum, the ungrateful bastards.

I lack even the strength to bring about the death I so crave.

Yes, of course, I'm clinically depressed. But, back in 1967, how am I supposed to know that?

To me depression is just a word: the superlative of sorrow.

At school, I've become the worst nightmare of many of my classmates, these girls who are so easily driven to tears and whose hatred only feeds my behaviour.

Flirting with their boyfriends, for instance, until they dump them and come chasing after me. Making fun of the fatsos, bullying the ugly ones and the slow-witted. Swearing at them like a sailor, using words so vile I wonder myself where I've picked them up, which bring them to the verge of hysteria, poor things.

Naturally, every now and then, there are phone calls and meetings with incensed parents and by now I know the principal's office better than my own room. But Papa keeps bribing him unashamedly; twice I've come upon Zoë running down the stairs to his office quickly and surreptitiously; when I ask her what she's doing there, she confesses everything. "Oh, baby, what possesses you to say such things?"

"Go and do the washing-up and leave me alone," I reply.

I'm so vile. I wonder if this hatred of myself can kill me like an overdose of poison.

If only.

Until one day the grownups' tolerance is exhausted.

It's very early in the morning and I'm dozing off in class – the result of yet another sleepless night – when our Greek Literature teacher, a sour, bony woman in her forties, scolds me for the umpteenth time with her penetrating voice.

"What's the matter, Horianos? Is today's lesson sending you to sleep?"

Some of the girls I've backstabbed start tittering.

And Katerina grows angry – mad – and suddenly erupts.

"No. I just can't stand looking at your ugly mug."

"Rude girl, what did you just say?" she demands and is about to get up from behind her desk.

But I leap from my own desk first, my long hair swinging like Medusa's head of snakes. "Sit down and shut your mouth, cunt-face! You don't wanna mess with me, trust me. All the guys who've ever seen you naked have turned queer. So just cut the crap and go find a blind donkey to get a piece of meat up your snatch, you dried-up spinster!"

The teacher opens and closes her mouth silently like a dying fish, and I go on abusing her, and when I run out of epithets, I start throwing things at her, while my classmates stare at me with eyes wide like poached eggs, terrified that they might accidentally trigger such an onslaught of violence themselves.

Eventually the teacher runs off panic-stricken, her shrieks echoing along the corridor: "She's crazy! She's going to kill me! Help!"

And I'm laughing with my sardonic, bitter laugh.

Then I laugh some more in the face of the principal.

"What's wrong, old geezer? Horianos didn't pay up this time?"

As expected, I am expelled. Cast off.

Now everyone at home is on my case. Finally, they decide that they'll just send me to a private high school for wealthy, problematic brats, the same one Cleo had attended – whose diploma Dad paid for through the nose. But I couldn't care less about all this.

Because by then I'm constantly occupied with little Minas, my two-year-old nephew whom I adore so much he sometimes makes me forget my endless grief.

You see, I forgot to mention the greatest source of misery that I enjoy with a hearty, sisterly *Schadenfreude:*

The wreck of my older sister's marriage.

The Horrors of Others: The Stain

Thus spoke Minas Horianos the day after his daughter Cleo's wedding: "Finally, the stain of this family is gone."

Why would a father utter such a hateful thing for the flesh of his own flesh? And what does it mean regarding the love he's shown to her?

Cleo was not like me – she was a different species of monster.

Firstly, by her appearance.

Despite Mum's superhuman (and exorbitantly pricey) efforts, despite all the doctors and the diets, Cleo grows fatter each year, until her siblings (namely Agis and I, who have suffered as kids from her cruelty) begin to call her *Fatty*, not only when they speak to one another, but even in front of their parents.

As in: "Where'd Fatty go?" Or: "Is Fatty on the prowl again?"

For here is the other face of the monster: to overcompensate for her bovine build in a field where she may excel – unlike school where she's the class ignoramus – or simply because it's in her nature, my sister is a shameless flirt, at least by the standards of the 60s.

Therefore: "She's out on the balcony again, showing off her udders like a whore who's just spotted the arriving navy fleet" (so says the affectionate father), or: "She goes out and shames us all with her conduct" (our prudish mother). In truth, the poor girl sits on the balcony and ogles the cutest passers-by, fantasizing about the man of her dreams who'll love her despite her obesity and save her from this house of misery – or she goes out for a soda with her girlfriends in popular downtown cafés, giggling about this and that famous actor, or clumsily flirting with one of the bored-looking waiters. However, the conscientious parents have to account somehow for the fact that their daughter is an untameable, practically illiterate and – to be honest – rather unlikeable creature. So they ascribe everything to her slutty nature, praying that the years go by, so they can marry her off before things get completely out of hand.

And, as they deserve, things do get out of hand, terrifyingly so.

His name is Takis, he is thirty-two, coming from some god-forsaken village and has been studying in Cologne, I don't even remember what, for about a thousand years, give or take. Our 'prize pig' (Dad again) meets him at a costume ball, where she goes dressed as Madame de Pompadour (a costume that allows her to show off her uncontainable boobs) with Zoë as a chaperone (yeah, right) dressed as a Hungarian beer-house maiden. I'm still laughing at this picture, even if I wasn't there to witness its full splendour, since at the time I was having a ball myself with all that suicidal depression matter.

Cleo is seventeen, but as if she's been ready for a lifetime, she ensnares Takis, tall, handsome and in a pirate's costume. They exchange some pleasantries, have a fantastic time and then go and do the unthinkable:

They elope!

That is, they sort of elope, because there's no money for an actual elopement, so they just spend the night in a hotel and the following morning Cleo returns home (where we are all beside ourselves with worry about her disappearance) arm-in-arm with her intended (so she'll be spared the beating she'd have got otherwise) and announces that she is betrothed to Takis.

Mama Rini doesn't collapse on the floor, doesn't writhe or pull her hair out as she'd normally do under the circumstances, because she has to be decorous and gracious in front of this strange man her daughter has brought home; furthermore the said strange man happens to be a complete and utter hunk (even I, the little shrimp, covet him and wonder how he could possibly be attracted to my bulldozer of a sister). So, our poor parents sit numbly in the drawing room, waiting for the in-laws to drive all the way from the village where they reside. At least they're not beggars, Mum whispers to me, after she's extracted the relevant information from Takis by plying him with liqueur; his father is a rich landowner, and he an only child, which is why he could afford so many years of 'studying' abroad.

And as the days go by and the preparations are under way to have the wedding as soon as possible (because everyone fears the unthinkable: that Cleo may already be pregnant), another disaster strikes: the couple plans to move back to picturesque Cologne until Takis gets his degree. "Oh, Mary Mother of God," my mother moans, "all my children are being taken away from me!"

The wedding goes as planned, costing a fortune. The newlyweds depart on a honeymoon with no fixed return date. The months go by, Takis is still pretending to be studying and Cleo to be a happily married wife and expectant mother, but since she's just a seventeen-year-old kid all alone and without speaking a word of German, deep down she's bored to death, so she's gobbling jar after jar of Nutella; and one fine morning, about seven or eight months after the wedding, the doorbell rings and I open the door and see an unknown woman who must weigh no less than three hundred pounds, and since I don't recognize my sister in this stranger's wide, ruddy face, I just shut the door again.

In the end we realize it's her and let her in, pretending to be over the shock (which we're not; the pregnancy makes her seem even more enormous), and we console her, Zoë, Mum and I, for Cleo is crying her pretty eyes out, wailing that she's fed up with her life and that Takis neglects her, that she curses the day she got married and wants a divorce. Our parents won't hear of it, of course – whoever heard of an eight-month-pregnant divorcée? It's out of the question. What needs to be done is that her husband must move back to Greece to take care of his wife in their brand-new and vast apartment that takes up an entire floor, part of Cleo's dowry. The in-laws agree –they're sick of supporting their good-for-nothing son – so Takis suddenly finds himself the manager of a store in Thessaloniki, while Cleo becomes the mother of the cherubic Little Minas.

This baby is a miracle: even Mama Rini's hard and heavy heart softens up when she sees him, which is fortunate, because she sees him all the time: Cleo has decided that maternity doesn't suit her, and that she wants to live her life to the fullest (that is, to start going out again with her old classmates whom she was wrong to have ditched in the first place). Therefore, Little Minas is in effect adopted by Zoë and me, since our mother behaves like the childless girlfriends of a new mother who can't wait to get away from the baby – for despite her grandson being good as gold, she's changed enough nappies for a lifetime (a declaration that has to be taken with a pinch of salt).

So, just as I was about to be swallowed up by despair over my undiagnosed sickness, Minas comes like the sun into my life. I push him along the esplanade, arousing a deluge of whistles and catcalls, because I'm quite the stunner even if I say so myself, with a fine figure and flaxen hair cascading down to my waist (a nightmare to wash, even for going to the toilet) and my usual attire: miniskirt, oversized shades, and that catnip for men: a baby in a pushchair.

Those precious, wonderful years I'll spend raising Minas, with what little maternal instinct I possess, will teach me for the first time a significant and oh so dangerous lesson: love for a child can fill up your emptiness, so that his or her life, filled with expectations and dreams, seems to become your own until you can no longer tell them apart. The child sleeps, and you dream; it eats, and you swallow.

In the meantime, Cleo gets divorced and remarries. This time, Papa Minas will alter his original declaration of paternal endearment:

"At last, this family's sewer has gone to stink up a different home."

But I'm already elsewhere.

For, during one of my outings with Little Minas, while seated on a corner table at a patisserie downtown, a strange man, a gorgeous man wearing an expensive suit, with light grey hair and amber eyes, has offered me a lighter, and in turn I've offered him my name and, a few moments later, my love.

Architecture of Chaos

His name is Andreas, and he is forty-eight – three times my age. A successful architect, wealthy, divorced but childless, incredibly handsome and as tender and loving towards me as a middle-aged baby who's just seen his much younger mother for the first time.

I'm not sure he believes I am eighteen, but I don't give a hoot; since my periods have started, I consider myself ready to enter womanhood, whatever that entails. Not that I'm being pressured in the slightest. Andreas is the perfect gentleman: he rushes to open the passenger door for you (he owns a dark green Alfa Romeo convertible), rises from his seat when he sees you coming, pulls back the chair for you, lights your cigarette, and with his every gesture and every word makes you feel that all his heart belongs to you.

Naturally, I'm head-over-heels in love, and dream of trips abroad and of a happy family of my own, oblivious to the impossibility of our affair. Furthermore, thanks to Andreas, who has restored some order to the chaos of my emotional world and nourished my soul with his love, I no longer fear large crowds or speeding cars or that I may go mad and kill myself – I'd be truly mad to kill myself when I have such a catch of a boyfriend.

At home, either they fail to notice any change in me because they're too busy trying to put some sense into Cleo who has abandoned her baby and whores around, or they simply don't care; so long as I'm not annoying them with my nervous condition or getting in trouble at school (where I barely set foot anymore), I'm free to date whomever I wish.

Now I must get a bit clinical.

Sex with Andreas is, to be honest, my first disappointment. It is just as tender and slow-paced and gentle as I had dreamed, filled with caresses, kisses and endearments, but it reminds me of an exquisitely cooked dish to which the chef, despite his talent, forgot to add a single grain of salt. The love fulfils some need in me, but doesn't satisfy my deeper, carnal hunger.

However, I've learned to react in the manner expected of me to his anxious queries as to whether I enjoy it and soon I became a highly convincing liar: I bat my eyelids, moan at the right moments and overall pretend to be the lascivious, wanton, ecstatic girlfriend I think a marvellous man like Andreas deserves. Besides, I've recently unearthed a copy of Joseph Kessel's *Belle de Jour* that Myron had stashed beneath his mattress and, aside from copying the sexual acts it portrays, I've realized that love – and the orgasm in particular – is no easy deal. It may require you to go to extremes, or you may never experience it until you try what your body really desires. Maybe I'm frigid, I think, and I give myself to Andreas with even greater abandon, determined to tell him the truth at some point, if I don't eventually reach the orgasm I so crave.

However, I'm distracted by another discovery. It takes a long time to dawn on me, because I'm not very experienced in matters of menstruation and the potential implications of its irregularities. I am pregnant. I say it over and over again to myself in order to believe it. *Katerina, you're pregnant.*

One would think that a young heartsick girl – especially one with my bizarre psychological condition – would view this pregnancy as a godsend, dreaming up a familial bliss.

No. I'm terrified. I can feel my childhood insouciance slipping away and I panic. I don't want to be a mother. I don't want to end up like Cleo and dump my baby into Zoë's care. I want to go back to being Little Katerina who read books and listened to records and played with her two-year-old nephew as if she were a baby herself.

Andreas agrees with me: he too is in a state of dread, since he wasn't planning on getting hooked with a wife and a baby of the same emotional maturity. Although he reassures me that if I want to keep it, he will support me wholeheartedly – and I believe he would have; he was a decent guy, the architect – I know him well enough to understand that the alternative he suggests with equal diplomacy (he has a friend who's an obstetrician and the operation is relatively painless and utterly safe) is the one we both prefer.

Maybe it shocks you, the ease with which I decided to have an abortion, especially in that day and age. Or you might suppose that the thought of this discarded child haunted me and became part of my illness.

Not at all.

For if I'd had that baby, I wouldn't have given birth to the son I had ten years later by my husband Tassos.

You can't know that, you'll say. Perhaps you wouldn't have had the exact same son, but another, or a daughter, and you might love them just the same or even more. Isn't that what the chaos theory says more or less? A butterfly flutters its wings, etc.

(Just now I remembered that Zoë used to call butterflies '*little souls*'. How fitting: the soul begins in the womb like a caterpillar and ends up as this beautiful butterfly, which longs to grow bigger and stronger so it can fly away free.)

So, no. Even if I cannot prove it, in the same way that I can't prove that God exists, I can swear with utter conviction in the name of my own personal God:

I could never love another child as I loved my son.

Insight

And what goes on in my life aside from my illicit love affair and my devotion to my nephew?

Lots of interesting things. For one, Agis, law graduate without the need for money that would drive him to practice his professional skills, has acquired over time friends and passions he shares with me. Hanging out with him, I'll get acquainted with films and books and music which I'll keep on devouring at night when he's not there and I'm left to roam the house where the adults sleep their peaceful sleep. At four and five in the morning he'll come upon me humming or dancing furiously around the room with my headphones on, or reading comic books and stifling my laughter with a fist in my mouth, or even baking a chocolate cake at six, in order to have a piece with my morning coffee an hour later. I live, and I'll go on living for many years to come, on two or three hours of sleep at most, something which I consider perfectly normal, a sign of my youth and my rebellious temperament. "Sleep is for the dead," I say, brimming with contempt for my snoring of my exhausted (and elderly) father, or for the muttering, coughing and groaning of Mum, who, either because of her missing lung or because she didn't have the life she'd dreamed of, had nights more restless than Macbeth.

I'm so full of vigour and have so much free time that in my last year of high school I even start showing up at the actual building, which up till then had never seen me in person, just the cheques for my tuition fees. With my preternatural stamina and the all-nighters I'm pulling, I manage to make up for the lost studying time and I become once more an A student – not that there was much competition, but still; my French, especially, has attained the level of a second mother tongue, and I often daydream of studying at the Sorbonne like Myron, or even better living the Parisian *dolce vita* on Horianos's money, dressing in haute couture like one of the models in *Paris Match* which I read from cover to cover. (In reality, I'll never see Paris with my own eyes.) For the time being, all I'm doing is dress rehearsals, wearing a beret, sipping Calvados and smoking those lethal filterless Gitanes.

Years later, reading day and night a massive textbook written by some American psychiatrist, my son will explain to me that this incredible, almost superhuman hyperactivity – which I still experience from time to time, in between abysses of depression – is also part of my disorder and is called hypomania. When I first hear the word in English, I think he's just said '*hippomania*' and I burst into laughter, imagining that the shrinks compare us to hippos because of our mad, indomitable strength; but no, the kid hurries to correct me, its etymology is the prefix hypo- and mania – the latter of which I've experienced first-hand (as do my husband and son) and I know it's nothing if not pathological.

But this is the problem, or rather the problem within the problem: when I'm all right, too all right, as I was at seventeen, when I got over an abortion and a breakup without shedding a single tear because I was too busy with a ton of things – so who gives a crap about the old man and his flabby flesh – or at thirty-three, when I stayed up all night dancing to Michael Jackson or the Pet Shop Boys blasting through the headphones, and I cooked four different main courses and ten kinds of dessert when the men of the house were away – so, when I'm going through the magical hypomania, I'm not aware that I am ill. I lack another psychiatric term: intellectual insight.

And here I was, always believing myself to be insightful.

It all boils down to the fact that, whenever I'm feeling fine, I stop taking my pills.

And when I crash once more, I take them by the handful.

Not even a hippo could handle that.

The Horrors of Others: The Second Wedding

But even though I was sick all those years, from the late 60s till the early 70s, my parents did not have a clue.

Because, once again, their attention as well as the concern of the entire family (that is, a middle-aged, unhappily married couple, poor Zoë who had to pick as a husband a latent homosexual on the lookout for a conveniently inexperienced country girl, and three deeply disturbed young siblings who either have a family disaster of their own under their belts – that would be Myron – or should be locked up, like Agis and me) is focused on Cleo.

A gay divorcée if there ever was one, after sending Takis off packing and unloading her kid on her younger sister, Cleo has decided that enough of the single-girl fun, she wants to settle down (again).

"Of course! By all means!" says Mama Rini, who couldn't be happier for she already has an eligible bachelor in mind – a friend of Papa Minas and owner of two huge stores in Athens. So what if he's a bit worn around the edges and a little flabby and father of two grown children from a previous marriage and only has about four hairs left on his head? She's got Cleo to marry off, a second-hand daughter with a toddler and a huge arse. And if everything goes smoothly, not only will she be forever ridden of her shameful excuse for a daughter, but she'll also have a legitimate reason to make impromptu trips to Athens as frequently as the average truck driver.

However, Cleo has different plans. She's already found her intended on her own. And if it's some charmer you're thinking, think again, or rather don't, because the guy is unthinkable.

His name being Koulis is the lesser offense.

The fact that he has four gold-capped teeth, all of them incisors, and whenever he opens his mouth it looks as if some tinfoil is stuck between his teeth, is slightly worse.

What makes him indescribable is that the guy is a loan shark and occasional fence, plus a complete and utter sleazeball, while the whole of northern Greece knows the stories of his various feats, having already done two stints at a nearby jail – the first time for smuggling leather jackets and the second for smuggling fur coats.

But what does it matter if he has a sordid past and 18-carat incisors when there's so much love in the air it looks like a swarm of gnats? And for some reason no one can fathom, Cleo melts at the sight of Koulis, as does Mum, only she, conversely, melts into tears and despair.

"Have you taken some kind of vow to bring all the riffraff home and marry them? Damn you, girl, the scum of the earth would look down on this man, he's a known criminal! Oh, Virgin Mary Mother of God, what sin have I committed that you see fit to punish me with such a daughter?"

This time Dad, despite his icy indifference to Cleo's future, also decides that she's gone too far, and threatens that unless she ends her affair with that vile crook immediately, he'll disown her and her beloved will never be found, because Dad will have him fitted with cement shoes and tossed into the Thermaikos Gulf to sleep with the shit-eating fishes.

Even Myron and Agis are recruited, being older brothers, to talk some sense into Cleo – switching roles as good cop and bad cop.

Finally, they manage to persuade Cleo; or rather Cleo is persuaded on her own, because despite the curfew enforced on her, during her walks out with Little Minas (whose pushchair, she has come to realize, is the best accessory for getting the attention of men – especially if you accompany it with a sob story about being a twenty-three-year-old widow with nothing but a son and an apartment as big as Texas to call her own), has met the man who is to become her second husband, father of her daughter and godfather to my son.

Vangelis the Arse-Snatcher.

The Man Who F***ed Too Much

Don't get the wrong idea about the man, Vangelis was anything but gay. Quite the opposite. His eyes popped out at the sight of any woman, no matter how plain or downright unattractive; he could find some alluring feature in every woman on earth.

So he falls in love with Cleo despite her blubber and in fact jokes, "Oh, I'd love to have a side of this tasty haunch!", and Cleo blushes and pretends she doesn't like it, and goes: "Don't, Vangelis, not in front of the boy!" even though the boy is sleeping serenely in my arms, oblivious of my guffaws.

Because Vangelis is one of those people who, even if they'd committed a crime against you, have such a wicked sense of humour, such capacity for taunts and self-deprecation, that you can't help loving him – the same way my sister loves him, even though he's not a looker: short, even shorter than Cleo (barely five feet tall, that is), pallid but hirsute as a bear, with a pointy nose and beady eyes. The cherry on top is his unimaginable wardrobe: polyester suits, vomit-green and gingivitis-pink, with huge lapels and bell-bottomed trousers as wide as twin skirts, shirts unbuttoned down to the navel, the better to show off the glint of the enormous golden cross that lies on the thick fur of his chest, and a mane of hair dyed black with shoe polish and coiffed in a pompadour so that he looks taller (or so he thinks). Oh, and he also grows his pinky nails, to show off his matching signet rings, as evidence that he does no manual labour – and also to reach those pesky boogers that get stuck too high up in the nostrils.

Vangelis is a shopkeeper, a man of villager stock and poor as a church mouse, and though at first our mother has fits of hysteria – this time she refuses to look even at a photo of her in-laws – he manages to earn Dad's trust with his attitude of a self-made, hard-working man (as if the first guy, the graduate slothful waste of a son-in-law, was any better) and ultimately he is allowed to marry Papa Minas's prize pig (a nickname Vangelis finds hilarious), a pressing event because Cleo just happens to be slightly pregnant again.

Everything would have gone just fine, but Vangelis, despite his charms, has one big flaw: whenever he sees a woman, he lights up. And although Cleo and we believe his flirting to be mostly harmless teasing and joking, that he's just pretends to be a womanizer and as soon as he becomes a husband and a father he will get over it, unfortunately, even after the birth of the tiny and adorable Irini, it turns out to be an incurable condition. The second some woman on the street makes eyes at him (or appears to), or turns around in response to his whistling (the scoundrel whistles too, penetratingly, like a shepherd gathering his flock), he locks up the new store his father-in-law bought him and chases after her. And he's completely inconsiderate: as if it weren't bad enough that he's out on the prowl every other night, even when Cleo is seven months pregnant and big as a house, he also takes many of his conquests for a coffee downtown, where, as is normal in any city as small as Thessaloniki, we've all run into him at one point or another.

Let me be perfectly honest. If we'd loved our sister more, we'd have taken him to task. However, this whole woman-hunt, combined with his whole buffoon persona, seems to us incredibly amusing, hilarious often; in private Agis confesses his undersexed heart's sorrow: "But how does he manage to lure them in, the bastard, looking like an aborted foetus and dressing as a clown?" Yet that's the way it is: if your only concern is chasing arse – flirting, necking, fucking – no matter how awful you look, one in every hundred will reciprocate the interest. He's even screwing his young employee Dora inside the store. He pretends to lock up and leave and then he goes back from the adjoining alley and the whole street resounds from Dora's squeals.

And the same thing goes on during the entire nine eventful – if not torturous – years of his marriage to Cleo. At some point, either out of despair or because she feels the rightful need to take revenge for all this cuckolding, our sister decides to spread the rumour that Vangelis is homosexual.

The first time she pretends to confess this thing to Agis and me, it's all we can do not to burst out laughing. Is she for real? Thessaloniki is small as a fart, and we've all run into Vangelis the Lech hand-in-hand with some chick. Who is ever going to believe her? But Cleo persists. First a friend of hers has seen him arm-in-arm with a sailor; then another friend saw him fellating a soldier in the back row of a cinema. Wild, extravagant concoctions, many of which she reveals to Vangelis himself, blaming his vice for the sorry state of their marriage.

Vangelis, however, pays her no heed. More than that, he starts to make fun of her. "And why should you care, honey? So long as your arse remains untouched, where's the harm in it?" Or: "That's the way I am – I can't get enough cock. Show me a guy and I'm all over him." Ergo his nickname – Vangelis the Arse-Snatcher – which, in later years of forgiveness and forgetfulness, even Cleo herself will be using, joking around, while Vangelis too is immensely fond of his moniker.

"Watch out, you filthy women, Vangelis the Arse-Snatcher is coming to plunder your men!"

The fun we used to have with that guy; we were in tears with his bullshit. That's why, when the time comes to baptize our son, it's a no-brainer: Vangelis will be his godfather, end of story, even if his marriage to Cleo is on its last legs.

And there's another trait of Vangelis which is equally, if not more, entertaining: he's so uneducated and possesses such a poor vocabulary, that whenever he's trying to describe something complicated, whatever noun or adjective or verb he can't remember becomes a version of '*you know*'.

"Jeez, Katerina, the other day I had this terrible row with your sis, you know, and I got so you-know-what-ed, you know."

Before the priest, before even my husband and son arrive, while the undertaker has still not delivered the coffin with my body to the cemetery, Vangelis the Arse-Snatcher will be the first person there to attend my funeral.

Schizophrenic Aged 39

He is an immigrant boy from Silivri on the outskirts of Istanbul, who, from the age of ten, worked like a slave to feed his uprooted family – his widowed mother and three younger siblings. At thirty, he'll find himself in Veria, northern Greece, selling wood for furniture. During his hard life, he's going to do anything and everything to make a living: drive a cab, play semi-professional football, work as an unskilled labourer in Düsseldorf. As if his fate weren't cruel enough, he'll be forever marked a communist because he read the 'wrong' newspaper, even though he's a moderate liberal: not so much a communist as a proletarian.

She's the daughter of a wealthy landowner from Naoussa, born with a bad hip, which gives her a lifelong limp and makes her extremely reserved and awkward.

They'll meet in 1949, get married in 1950, and in 1955, after a difficult Caesarean, she'll give birth to her first son, a swarthy, chubby baby of ten pounds. Four years later, after an even more difficult Caesarean, she will have her second son, who'll weigh even more. Back then, the women who bred only sons were called *she-dragons*.

The family, despite the deprivations – because the father-in-law is a royalist and dislikes his Commie son-in-law – will be a happy one, even if both parents play favourites with their firstborn. It's hard and wrong, but at that time this sort of inequality was very frequent.

The older son will have just entered puberty when his mother, at 39, becomes pregnant again. During those years, a pregnancy at that age was considered perilous, and yet she insists on keeping the third baby, hoping that the Good Lord will finally give her the daughter she so craves.

Due to an unknown complication, the foetus will die a few days after she enters the eighth month of her pregnancy and the mother will only realize it a little later by the stench of sepsis that suddenly wafts from between her legs.

In danger of septicaemia, she's carted off to the hospital beside herself with terror – because she still believes her baby can be saved, *must* be saved – but, as luck would have it, she is submitted not only to an urgent abortion but to a complete hysterectomy. When she recovers, something inside her feels broken, torn. Who knows? Maybe it had been torn all along, hiding behind her shyness and taciturnity, so that it remained undetected by other people. The diagnosis will be *paranoid schizophrenia*.

Another clinic; although in this one she's strapped to her bed, and when the injections don't do the trick anymore, she's submitted to ECT twice a week. She barely escapes having a lobotomy which a couple of doctors recommend, being specialists in that barbaric thing called *psychosurgery*, because her husband won't hear of it: he demands to take her home and be her carer.

It will be much harder than he imagines, at times inhumanly so. His psychically devastated wife oscillates between periods of frightening apathy – sometimes just sitting immobile for hours and staring into the void – and outbursts of fury and aggression towards herself and others, based on paranoid ideas: that her sons conspire to murder her because they're jealous of their little sister, that her husband is at one time a burglar who's broken into her home to rape her, at another time Lucifer in the flesh.

Those two boys will go through hell, not knowing how to cure a mother who doesn't even seem aware of their love for her. And the older son especially will care and worry for her his entire life. As a result, he will be an infinitely affectionate man, a protector of the weak, with just one flaw: an utter despair (as an echo of his traumatic adolescence) in the face of mental illness. He'll be forever a victim to this ambivalence: on the one hand he's secretly attracted to unstable women, and on the other he's terrified of their potential helplessness and a lifetime of caring for a sick wife.

My beloved Tassos, please forgive me. You had no idea.

But neither did I.

A Nanny and a Whore

Anno Domini 1972.

By such a coincidence that makes you want to believe in fate, Tassos and his family have moved from Veria to Thessaloniki, where his father works and Tassos is a student of dentistry – in fact, they're renting an apartment in the building where Cleo lives, just one floor up.

The young Dr Hatzopoulos is twenty-one and dangerously gorgeous: tall, dark, with shoulder-length ebony hair contrasting with his crisp white shirts and cream-colored jackets. Women young and old are after him with a vengeance, and every now and then he's shacking up with one of them – but soon he's back at his place to care for his mother, who's turned into a breathing piece of furniture after all the anti-psychotics she's ingested: one day she has complete comprehension, the next her mind switches off like a light bulb.

And one day, when he's out on the balcony having a cigarette, he looks down and notices a girl unlike anyone he's ever seen: even though miniskirts and platform shoes are a dime a dozen, this one has golden hair as long as Rapunzel's, cascading from the third-floor railing as she leans over to hang some baby clothes to dry – Tassos wants to run his fingers through that hair, inhale its scent – while at the same time she's singing some French song. A Frenchie, huh?

Tassos wastes no time: he goes and finds the building busybody (his younger brother, who knows everything), and learns that the entire third floor belongs to a rich young woman on her second marriage and mother of two. And the babe? The brother has no idea. "I think she's the nanny or something – but I can't swear on it." So she's really a foreigner, hot stuff.

However, girls are aplenty and Tassos doesn't want to fall in love with a foreigner who'll leave and break his heart – he's two months from graduation, he needs to focus – so the crush is forgotten for nearly two years.

Whereupon, in the summer of '74, while waiting to get drafted in the autumn, he decides to take a chance and rings the doorbell of the lady downstairs, because the other day he spotted the girl again.

Cleo opens the door and is inordinately polite – would he care for a refreshment? A vermouth, perhaps? Some fig preserve? On the subject of the blonde, though, she's extremely vague. "She's the kids' English governess," she finally says. "Doesn't speak a word of Greek."

Why would my sister tell such a lie? Because she's jealous of me, and she doesn't want Little Katerina to bag such a handsome neighbour. (She, too, has stumbled on the misery game: since she can't be happy herself, she'll do everything in her powers to make sure no one else is happy either.)

But Tassos doesn't lose heart. He might be self-taught in English, but he's spent so many summers working in various island resorts, he's fluent enough to flirt. So, the first time he runs into the babe on the stairwell, he gives her the standard lines: "How do you do? Do you like Greece?" etc etc.

I burst out laughing – for one, because I too have fancied the heartthrob neighbour for years now, and also because of his English.

"I'm Greek, darling. Born and bred here in Thessaloniki!"

He seems a bit startled; nevertheless, he regains his composure at once and suggests going for a walk on the seafront and stopping at a nice patisserie (that's how he first wins me over: the chocolate-swarthy lover who wants to treat me to a slice of chocolate cake).

"I have to babysit my nephew and niece," I say. "Same time tomorrow?"

He seems perplexed again – he thought I was the nanny – but he eagerly accepts.

All this happens on Friday, July 19th – just a day before the Turkish invasion of Cyprus.

Our first time together will be soaked in bloodshed.

August will find us in the throes of early love: kisses and caresses and nights sweet as honey. I had no clue what love felt like before Tassos, my raven-haired beau, whose every touch makes me open like a flower.

As September looms ahead, faced with the twenty-eight months in the army that will take him away from me, he decides to do the right thing: talk to my parents, and ask for my hand in marriage – or at least in engagement, until he's through with the army.

It is the first time that my parents are thrilled by the future spouse one of their kids has chosen: Papa Minas because this youth seems hardworking and level-headed, street-smart and tough, and Mama Rini because at long last a doctor (dentists are doctors, right?) has graced her humble abode. Compared to the older one's collection of scum, this fine young man glows like an obsidian sculpture in her eyes.

The next day I meet my own in-laws who welcome me with just as much joy and warmth, as the daughter they always longed for. But once I leave, Chryssoula, Tassos's mother, takes her son aside and confesses to him her only concern.

About a week earlier, she says, the downstairs neighbour, the fat lady with the kids, waited for her in the stairwell to warn her that her son should steer clear of Katerina, because although she's her sister and loves her dearly, the girl is the worst kind of man-eater ever created, and has bedded half the men in Thessaloniki, so that her parents are trying to marry her off to prevent a scandal – and she, as her sister, couldn't in all conscience bear it if an eligible bachelor like Tassos threw his life away by marrying that slut. "And, Mrs Hatzopoulos, don't discount the possibility of her having caught who-knows-what diseases!"

Tassos won't be troubled even for a second: laughing it off, he'll reassure his mother that Katerina is all right, and in fact a virgin until recently (even though I've told him all about Andreas and the abortion – it was my moral duty, for all the love he gave me).

And later on we'll laugh together at Cleo's outrageous lies. Another person in my shoes would have written her off – but I'm so in love I feel magnanimous, and in truth I feel sorry because she's so miserable that she gets her kicks out of struggling to deprive others of happiness, even her own sister. Tassos, of course, will nurse a lifelong dislike for her, and with good reason. "If I believed that cow's lies, we wouldn't be together right now."

And they say blood is thicker than water. Well, so is shit.

Before the motherland steals him away from me, he'll give me my all-time favourite record: Hadjidakis's *Magnus Eroticus*.

The Horrors of Others: And What About the Junta?

This is how the seven years under the military junta pass in the house of Horianos.

We embrace, as usual, our father's opinion: he despises all high-ranking military men out of an undying hatred for his brass-hat older brother. The dictator and his buddies are *'bad dirt'* to him.

He harbours the exact same scorn for the Greek royal family (*Those German layabouts, a pox on them!*) despite the fact that his wife, for reasons of decorative kitsch, is a naïve royalist.

Georgios Papandreou is *'that louse who abandoned his wife and ran off with that cock-sucking whore of an actress'* (in the idiosyncratic moral universe of Papa Minas, every woman of loose morals is a round-the-clock cocksucker), and as for the Communists, they're *'those dirty Russians' patsies'*.

The only statesman he supports, indeed admires passionately, is Konstantinos Karamanlis. His love for him is probably founded on the fact that he, too, is a self-made giant from the depths of rural Greece and that his origins are evident (as in Horianos himself) in his heavy village accent. His pro-Karamanlis politics prompts his wife (who most likely had the hots for Karamanlis) to order a marble bust of the great statesman, which stands in pride of place in the main hallway, among copies of famous Renaissance and Baroque paintings.

As for the Horianos siblings, our politics are as vague and irrational as those of all children who grow up in wealth, and to whom the demands of the people are something so alien, it can only be conceived symbolically.

Myron, for instance, is incensed that he didn't stay in Paris, where he imagines he'd be best buddies with Melina Mercouri and the crème de la crème of the expatriated resistance.

Cleo's opinion on politics is so uninformed that if you asked her who Papadopoulos was, she'd probably say, "Ooh! The one who makes the cookies, right?"

Agis, on the other hand, mainly because of his love for the music of Theodorakis, feels he is a left-winger, even if only in theory; in fact, when Mum is away, he often invites fellow graduates home – they too are crypto-leftists of wealthy Thessaloniki families – and they all hole up in our old room to listen to the revolutionary *Romiosyni*, with Zoë in the role of the butler, preparing and serving them sandwiches and vermouths. These gatherings stop after a neighbour, eavesdropping on the scandalous songs these unpatriotic youths are playing, informs Mum about them, although Mama Rini isn't so much worried about whether our family is stigmatized as left-wing, more that one of these unshaven hoodlums might steal one of her porcelain shepherd figurines.

I, for one, am an ardent lover of Hadjidakis (right-wing in the narrow minds of many people), and I'm sixteen and madly in love with the architect, so I'm living in my own blissful world. (And I'm not using this as an excuse – in the years to come, many times I shall feel that it was unforgivable of me and after the fall of the military junta I'll listen again and again the record made during the bloody and heroic Athens Polytechnic uprising, and go to concerts and marches and demonstrations, trying to make up for my youthful indifference. The only thing I will never do, as a matter of principle, is fill my son's heart with my own regrets about my nonexistent left-wing past.)

Perhaps the sole bona-fide Communist in the family is Zoë, because of her dating '*that Pinko sodomite*' (my father's own ever-sweet words) that will mould her into a lifetime voter for the Greek Communist Party. Although I still recall her rather baffling comment that went against her supposed convictions:

"Thank the Lord we never became like those poor Russian Commies," which she always accompanied with a vigorous crossing of herself.

Only one thing bugs me: whatever happened to that bust of Karamanlis?

Kisses Thick with Lipstick

The twenty-eight months we'll spend apart, Tassos and I will write dozens, maybe hundreds, of letters to each other, brimming with yearning and loving desire. Mine resemble a schoolgirl's letters to imaginary boyfriends: written on small sheets of pink stationery, often adorned with hearts and doves and a lot of embarrassing things, filled with endearments and underlined words. Beneath my name, I sign with a kiss applied with a heavy layer of lipstick, so the trace of my lips may reach my beloved still moist, for I think of him pressing his own full, gorgeous lips to the paper.

Tassos' letters, on the contrary, aside from his breathtakingly handsome handwriting which I can't get enough of – letters as black and perfectly shaped as his eyes – are more mature, more adult and daring; without ever straying to the pornographic, they make his lust for me so plain, so tangible, that often at night, while I'm struggling in vain to fall asleep, I press them against my bosom or place them gently between the warm crevice of my thighs.

However, on my first visit to the camp, his looks are disturbing: his beautiful long hair has been cropped and, having lost at least ten pounds, his angular face reminds me of a prisoner of war – which is, sadly, not too far from the truth.

Because, even though the year is 1975, the army is still rife with countless filthy junta sympathizers who hate it that they've lost all their comforts and privileges. Seeing on my beloved's file that his father was a Communist, they submit him to unimaginable torments. Noticing, appalled, that whenever he takes a step he struggles not to wince, I interrogate him and he reveals that his bastard of a lieutenant forces him to make the rounds of the camp on his knees, and sleep sitting upright with his heavy boots on, so that his feet have been deformed by the swelling. During his first leave we'll spend endless hours in Mum's resplendent private bathroom (Mama Rini was so fond of her son-in-law, she'd even let him sleep in her bed if he wished to) washing my sweet Tassos' bloody feet with a soft sponge and baby soap and it's all I can do not to burst into tears.

That is when I'll make a vow: if I ever have a son, I'll never let him serve in the army. They'll have to go over my dead body to take him from my steely grasp.

Ridicule and Panic

The years go by, the day of our wedding arrives: Sunday, 18 February 1977, at the cathedral.

The photos confirm it: it's a ridiculous ceremony.

I'm wearing a ridiculous wedding dress with long sleeves like lengths of curtain drooping all the way to the floor, and my dark-blond hair is amassed under a lace cap that would look well on a religious cult neophyte – as Agis will comment in a low voice, giving me the day's first good laugh, it resembles the ball suspenders Mum used to buy for Dad's itch-prone testicles.

Tassos is wearing a decent-enough suit, yet his enormous, funereal-purple bowtie, combined with his massive moustache which threatens to assume the size of a ceiling fan's paddles, makes the whole thing ridiculous as well.

Our parents are also ridiculously overdressed: the mothers, trying to outdo one another, have laden themselves with every piece of fur and jewellery they own, so they look like middle-aged statues of the Virgin Mary on some Mexican Catholic feast – oh, and they're both sporting brand-new, blinding-white dentures, courtesy of my own sweet Tassos. As for the fathers, they are striving to endure as stoically as possible the lengthy ceremony, because they both despise passionately anything that has to do with priests and religion, plus they're both forced by their wives to wear shiny silk suits. Petros, my father-in-law, also has a moustache, greyish but just as huge as his son's, while Dad, sixty-seven now, looks older and more dilapidated than ever; the way he keeps batting his eyelids slowly, I fear he might actually doze off standing there. It wouldn't be the first time.

My siblings stand across from me. Myron with his second wife Vivi (a wonderful girl and amazing architect), Cleo arm-in-arm with Vangelis the Ass Snatcher – their marriage is on the verge of utter collapse, but they're both smiling so widely you'd think they're waiting their turn to get married all over again, with Little Irini dressed up as a flower girl, although she's barely old enough to stand. Finally, Agis, stands next to his nineteen-year-old wife Ritsa, who, although she hadn't initially received the favour of the court (since Mama Rini, forgetting her own humble youth in the shack and Dad's uncouthness, had considered it a staggering personal defeat when she found out Ritsa's father was a farmer from a small village in Thessaly), will become Agis's guardian angel: it is thanks to that remarkable woman's love that my dear brother is still alive and hasn't joined me where there is no pain, no sorrow, nor pretty much anything, really.

I could have – silently, inwardly – enjoyed the numerous touches of the guests' collective ridiculousness, since they have gathered here from the farthest reaches of provincial Greece and are even more outrageously bedecked in splendour than our families, but my amusement runs into a sky-high, impenetrable wall of panic, which keeps on rising and rising before me.

Because, it's one thing to have walks and drives and necking in the car and love from a distance until we each go home to our respective parents, but the thought that, as of tonight, he and I are moving to the same house, where we're expected to spend the rest of our lives in love and harmony, invites unutterable panic. And it's not so much the living together that terrifies me – after all, I do want to be with him all the time – but then every morning my one and only is supposed to get up early and go to work in the hospital that has just hired him, and I'll have to stay home all alone and do – what? Laundry? Housework? Cooking? In theory I know how to do all these things, but the thought of the empty hours I'm destined to spend in an unfamiliar apartment, away from the place I've always called home and Zoë and my parents, makes me weak with fear. If anyone looks at the wedding photos, they can clearly see it: my smile is more forced and fake than a politician's poster photo.

And as if this mountain of anxiety wasn't bad enough, at one point the dirty old goat of a priest (in my eyes all priests are dirty old goats, like my grandfather who let his own son contract TB just so he could humiliate him) intones, "*And may the Lord grant this woman fruit of the womb*", and my panic multiplies; so much so that I can barely contain it and resist the urge to toss the bouquet aside and make a run for it in my wedding-dress-cum-living-room-curtain.

Because, a few months back, one fine morning of December 1977, I'd woken up with an agonizing pain in my stomach and I'd rushed to the bathroom where, slipping on the blood that was leaking from my womb, I had my first miscarriage. And the horrible day when I lost my second child brings to my mind the first one, the one I aborted when I was sixteen, and suddenly I'm overcome with terror that God will punish me for my ghastly adolescent trespass and I will lead a life of infertility and childlessness, miscarrying little bits of unborn children into the toilet bowl.

The psychic storm of the wedding is a harbinger of the mild depression to which I'll succumb the following month – so that we have to cancel our honeymoon in Venice (lucky for me, or else I'd have to confess to my Tassos, who's loved aeroplanes since he was a boy and one day will become a light aircraft pilot himself, that the mere thought of boarding a plane makes me want to weep with fear), and instead we go to the northern town of Kastoria for a few days, where I'll categorically refuse Tassos's offers to buy me a fur coat – for I read in *Paris Match* about the animal-rights activism of Brigitte Bardot whom I've idolized since I was a girl; I might even have had a slight teenage crush on her.

As a result of my post-wedding depression, February and March go by without a single occasion of intercourse, something that Tassos handles with angelic forbearance. However, on the night of April 2nd, on my birthday, I decide that I owe him one night of passion in my arms as a small gift for his patience and affection.

And, despite all my fears, I conceive on that very night.

Pregnancy on the Rocks

The moment the disaster happens, we're lying on the living-room sofa watching TV. I can't remember exactly what was on – all I recall is a commercial for canned milk.

On top of my humongous belly lies an ashtray (despite my gynaecologist's advice, I haven't managed to quit the damn things), and next to it, tied around my neck with string, hangs an icon of Saint Nectarios.

Since when have I, who never had any dealings whatsoever with anything remotely religious, started wearing something that would look over the top on an archbishop?

The answer is quite simple: since last year's miscarriage, I'm so terrified I may lose this child as well that I'm seeking help even from sources which until now I considered inane, if not entirely nonexistent.

And the way Saint Nectarios has come into my life is also oddly familiar. Of course I knew of him by hearsay – he was the last saint to be canonized by the Orthodox Church, and countless Greeks invoke his name – but the first time I decided to look further into the case of this particular holy man was after a talk I had with my father-in-law, Petros.

"You know," he said to me, "in order to appreciate what an illustrious family you've joined – never mind that we're paupers and still renting in our old age – I should tell you I am a proud compatriot of Saint Nectarios."

Being bookish, I went to a religious bookstore and read up on the subject. And I found out that indeed, Anastassios Kephalas, as was his real name, was born in Silivri, just like old Mr Hatzopoulos. A double omen: the saint was also my Tassos's namesake.

And having read about the host of miracles attributed to him and about the crowds that flock to the island of Aegina – where he led his frugal, Saint-Francis-like life – to listen to his living heart that is said to still beat from inside his tomb (this I actually find kind of scary), I decide to make a sacred vow to his grace.

Saint Nectarios, I pray, *please keep my baby safe, and I'll come on my knees to kiss your marble tomb.* Of course by then my knees were swollen to twice their normal size (I'll put on sixty pounds during my pregnancy, greedy sow), and I knew that in order for a vow like that to work you were supposed to name your child after the saint in question. But I've already fallen in love with my father-in-law's name: my son is going to be named Petros – I'm certain it's going to be a son – and so as not to displease the saint, I seal the vow by hanging his icon around my neck, swearing I won't take it off for a second until my boy lies safely in my arms.

And up until that night, the fateful night of June 20th, 1978, Nectarios has kept his promise: no bleeding, no pain, not even nausea: Katerina is a pregnant doll, only I'm eating for ten and the doctor has chided me repeatedly: "You silly woman, you'll have eclampsia and explode! For God's sake, cut back on the nosh!" but I'm not going to listen to that nobody doctor when I have an actual saint on my side, whose heart still beats inside the tomb, and one of these days I'm going to press my ear against the marble and be scared shitless.

Therefore, we're all cool and relaxed when the room begins to shake.

I've never lived through an earthquake before and I let out a piercing scream: "Tassoooooooos!" as if it were his fault for letting out a big one.

Suddenly the couch heaves and tosses me onto the floor, as if it's fed up of my huge buttocks on its back, and the shelves across the room disgorge everything on top of them to the floor as well: vases, glasses, the TV, the record player; even the cupboards are wrenched open and spill out pieces of knitting and embroidery – a real mess, and on top of that the ceiling has split from side to side, framed paintings are crashing onto the floor making a hellish racket, and I'm still lying on the carpet like a beached orca, shrieking.

An eruption of an indescribable panic inside me make my old anxiety attacks look like child's play, because this is what they call an act of God, and it seems he's bent on ripping us to pieces. And just as I used to do back in the day whenever terror seized me, I crawl to a heap of fallen bottles to find something to drink, even though booze hasn't touched my lips for the whole four months of my pregnancy – this is the end of the world, who gives a hoot what the doctors say?

And damn my luck, all of the bottles have been smashed save the whisky and I hate whisky (it's the cheap stuff too that smells like insecticide), but this is not the time to be picky, because Tassos is yelling at me from the hall, which is already filled with packed suitcases (when did he manage to pack, the blessed man? He's born for disasters!) saying we must leave before the building collapses and squashes us flat.

Beside myself with horror, but with the bottle firmly clasped in my hand, I tumble down the stairs from our fourth-floor apartment, and we run out the front door into the courtyard that's already covered with a cloud of cement dust, bolt into the red Peugeot Myron had given us as a wedding present because he'd got a new one, and we take to the streets without even knowing where to go.

Or maybe Tassos knows, because we head downtown, where our parents live as well as his brothers and all of my clan. We inch along the choked-up roads, and as we approach the White Tower, we see Papa Minas and Mama Rini. I actually recognize them from my mother's wig, which in her panic she's stuck on her head the wrong way around and looks like a Spartan-helmet-meets-Goldilocks.

They cram into the car with us, Mum crying because some plaster fell from the ceiling and ruined her Bukhara carpet (no, I wasn't drunk yet, the woman was actually lamenting her rug), while Dad is cursing me: "You lousy drunk, you're gonna get my grandson hammered in your belly"), and a little way down the street, here come my in-laws in their nightclothes. After we pick up my brother-in-law Paschalis as well, we go all the way back to our apartment, because the building is newer and supposedly safer.

In the meantime, insecticide smell or not, I've gone through half the whisky, and I couldn't be happier: "Hey, guys, now we're all together, let's go for a drive to Baxe-Tsiflik! It's such a lovely night!" And after that I conk out, and God knows how they got me up the stairs, but in any case I slept like the dead until twelve the next day, oblivious to the shaking from the aftershocks all night.

The following month we will be a nightmare of moving back and forth: from the tents they've set up in the park near the White Tower, to our summer place in Platamon, and from there to Veria to some relatives of Tassos and back again to Thessaloniki, which, having lost nearly thirty souls to the big earthquake, is still picking up its pieces.

The contractor for the building spares no expense to make it quake-resistant with extra cement beams, and repairs all the damaged apartments. By August our home is the safest place on Earth and we manage to replace everything that was destroyed with a little help from Dad.

Even months after my son is born, I won't touch a drop of alcohol.

I even manage to quit smoking and go easy on the food, for after the scare I got, which will leave me with a lifelong terror of earthquakes, I need to protect my son as best as I can.

And of course, let's not forget the Saint who saved us all.

Nativity

January 2nd, 1979, and since eight in the evening a powdery, fairy-tale snow has been falling from the sky.

Tonight it's precisely nine months since the night of my son's conception, and although the doctor has assured me many times that a lot of women give birth after they reach full term and that's perfectly natural, I know for certain:

I was born on April 2nd, Tassos was born on November 2nd, and tonight, on January 2nd, my son is going to be born.

Even though it's the first pregnancy I've carried to term, and I'm not having the C-section the doctor suggested, I'm serene, beatific, convinced that everything will be just fine.

So, when I feel the first contraction around ten o' çlock, despite the stab of pain I turn to Tassos and nonchalantly say: "Go and fetch my things. I'm giving birth."

Unlike himself, he is so panic-stricken you'd think he was the one about to pop one out. He's running back and forth like crazy, once to bring the suitcase, a second time to get his wallet, a third time to grab the camera – oh, because I forgot to tell you that whatever Tassos loves in this world (above all, me and my belly) he photographs it all the time incessantly, mercilessly, until you're fed up and you yell: "Enough, give me a break! How would *you* feel if you'd been trying to fart for a full hour and had me taking photos all the while?"

We leave the house at ten-fifteen, we get to the clinic at ten-twenty, and at a quarter to eleven I give birth, practically with a single push – even though my angel is a chubby baby of eight pounds – to my son Petros.

In the meantime, outrageous scenes have taken place. Inside the delivery room, for instance, I'm there with my feet spread wide and Tassos is poised at dead centre, waiting to immortalize our child the second he shows his face. I can't begin to describe the obscenities I hurl at him – is he totally nuts, looking for the best close-up of my twat while I'm in agony – but he manages to capture his son still bloody from the womb before he even opens his eyes. Or later on, when the doctor orders me to rest, saying they'll bring the baby up from the infant care ward tomorrow, because I need to sleep and it's unwise for a mother to see the baby a few moments after she's been through the painful process of labour – he knows all about my history of depression and wants to protect me from a potentially acute case of post-partum depression – but I'm not even listening, I'm yelling that if he doesn't bring me my Petros to hold him in my arms, I'll get up, go to the operating room, grab the butcher knife he used to slice me open like a turkey so the prize baby could come out, and cut his throat and the throat of that dog-ugly nurse he's bonking on the side, thinking nobody's the wiser, when everyone can see she's practically drooling over his double chin. Oh yes – you see, the shot of tranquilizer they've given me hasn't kicked in at all. My maternal instinct has turned me into a lioness, invulnerable to any drug.

So, a few minutes later, Petros is resting on my bosom and then, with eyes shut, he finds my breast and begins to suckle with greedy determination.

And even if, in following years, I found myself many times in a much, much worse Hell than the one with which they threaten the victims of suicide, at least I know what Heaven is like. It is that night – the moment Petros lets go of my breast after he's had his fill, opens his eyes and looks at me.

The Melancholy Breast

Those first forty days of motherhood I only recall as a splendid, endless dream. I never leave my son for a single second – even when Tassos takes him from me and puts him in his crib to sleep, I reach over with my forefinger extended and he wraps his tiny fist around it. I can stay sleepless for hours on end, just so I won't disturb this gentle touching.

But when I wake up one morning, something's changed. I feel a weight pressing down on me, a darkness clouding my thoughts. And just like that, my breasts run dry; in vain does my beloved Petros suckle and whimper, biting my nipple so hard that it bleeds.

Fortunately, having read all about postpartum depression, I know I need help. I don't want to spend a single moment without my son, yet I realize I'm not capable of caring for him on my own, not even for the five or six short hours when Tassos is away at work.

So, on that very day, we pack and move for a while to my old room in my parents' place. Papa Minas has turned it into a married couple's bedroom with a king-size bed and a brand-new crib for his grandson.

This is my son's first miracle: my eighty-year-old father, that indomitable stony-faced redneck, who never had a kind word for anyone in his life, melts at the sight of his grandson even though he's not named after him. He is transfixed, transformed. So, whenever I feel tired or don't want to hold him anymore because I think I'm about to cry and don't want to upset him, he never lets Mum be a grandmother even for a second: he grabs him tight and the baby, feeling the love that overflows from the old man's heart, sleeps as peacefully as if cradled in the arms of his guardian angel.

This almost pathological obsession with Mr Petros, as he calls him with a big smile (when did my father learn how to smile?) will provoke the unspoken, if justified, fury of my siblings. For one thing, because they never received such affection from Papa Minas (neither themselves nor their babies), and on the other hand because Dad, extreme in everything, takes things too far. Like on the afternoon when Cleo visits with the seven-year-old Irini, who is overjoyed to finally meet her baby cousin; but at that moment Petros is asleep under his grandpa's unmoving gaze and Irini's gleeful shriek wakes him, so Dad goes to the kitchen, grabs the biggest knife he can find and starts chasing his granddaughter around the house to slaughter her, saying, "She woke up the baby, the little whore!" I take my sister's side, of course, and yell at him for getting angry with the little girl and scaring her to death, but deep down inside a wicked part of me feels proud as hell.

And there's another miracle. Either because of the love that suffuses the house like a nourishing fragrance or because of the safety I feel back in my childhood home – no matter the cause, the depression subsides day by day until it becomes a vague kind of sadness and then departs for good.

But we do stay a few extra days, if for no other reason than because Papa Minas, learning that his son-in-law has been paying for the exorbitantly expensive baby formula out of his own pocket – and despite Tassos's stern refusal, who is unbelievably proud and never wants to feel beholden to anyone – he's gone and bought enough formula for a legion of infants.

And now that I'm well and in the night I don't turn my back on Tassos, we lie in bed with Petros between us and we joke around, betting on whose side the baby will turn first. Naturally, the baby will always turn towards its mother, but seeing how it saddens Tassos that his son couldn't care less for him, I suggest we change sides. And indeed, as soon as we do, Petros turns towards his father, and I fall asleep under his adoring gaze. Now it is my turn to feel sad.

Your children turn you into a child.

And a child, unfortunately, is prone to competition, petty jealousy and resentment.

Even a grown-up child.

The Words

How fast the days and months go by! How quickly he grows! At six months, he already looks like a toddler, so much so that other mums on the street ask me sometimes: "Such a big boy still in the pushchair?" That's how I want my angel to be: strong and healthy and well-fed on anything that nourishes body and soul.

I barely have time to think about myself – if I do have a self outside Petros – and depression couldn't be further from my mind: when I've got a treasure like this, I'm not going to sit around and mope like an imbecile.

I'm afraid that I've been neglecting Tassos, but I have no choice; I can't very well be having sex when my child is sleeping next to me. Of course, there are so many rooms available. But still, I don't know; I don't miss it, I don't *need* it as I did before. Back then, my body was meant for Tassos: to caress and kiss it, to do whatever he wanted with it. Now, it's like a vessel, a casing: an empty embrace waiting for Petros to wake up and fill it.

A little before he's eleven months old, on Saint Catherine's Day, he takes his first steps. I'm shrieking and clapping my hands, and Tassos is taking pictures and hides so Petros will go after him. He's wearing a long white nightgown, and his brand-new red booties excite his curiosity as much as the surrounding world which has suddenly become lower – when he's not traipsing left and right with arms extended and his mouth of four tiny teeth wide-open in a drooling cry, he stands, wobbling, and examines with avidly staring eyes these red things that have swallowed up his feet.

In the meantime, as early as August, he's started to talk. And not just random, isolated words; he forms entire sentences, specific orders, the little devil. For instance, because his father's the one who most often operates the record player, cleaning up the dust from the vinyl and placing the needle on the right track, etc., whenever he wants to listen to music (which is all the time; he seems as hungry for it as for food), he points at the Kenwood and says, "*Tatso, moosy!*" Or, because he's crazy about banana baby food, he shouts at me, "*Mama, bana!*" And so on. He even distinguishes between outings, asking for "*Jo!*" (Peugeot) when he wants a car ride, and "*Mama, shair!*" when he feels like going out on the pushchair. He even has a favourite song: 'Rasputin' by Boney M, which he asks for, swinging his head like a metronome and yelling, "*Ra! Ra! Ra!*" But the moments that utterly drive me mad with love, the moments I just want to eat him up, is when I'm in a different room and he, judging by the distance that a simple *Mama* will not suffice but that some more decisive call is needed, calls like his father, "*Katilina?*" and then, more forcefully, "*Kati!*"

I'm so proud of these words, filled with awe – as if it's God Himself who speaks to me. I make Tassos bring his tape recorder from work and I make a tape devoted exclusively to Petros's first utterings. And sometimes, when the two men of the house are sleeping peacefully, I sneak into the living room, put the headphones on, and listen to this tape for hours on end, feeling my insides swoon to the sound of this most exquisite music.

I try not to believe that Petros is God's chosen creature, a wunderkind of some kind, because it's too early and I don't want to jinx it. Furthermore, I've read that kids with an unusually high IQ may have trouble adjusting and socializing at school, and above all else I want my child to be happy. Brilliant, of course, and more special than all the children put together, but happy. I'm not asking for much.

I also have another embarrassing habit, though why should I be embarrassed? I imagine many mothers do that: after I bathe him and towel him up and sprinkle him with talcum powder and he's as soft and fragrant as a loaf of soft bread fresh from the oven, I bite his tiny feet gently and if he reaches up to me, I swallow his fist saying, "Mmmm!" as if I'm about to actually eat it up, and this makes him laugh, so I suckle to my heart's content his tiny fist with these perfect little fingers and their fingernails small as grains of rice.

That's why God exists: who else could have made a hand like this?

A Bookish Life

It goes without saying that every decision I make, aside from my own instinct, is based on the books on motherhood, child psychology and child-rearing which I keep on devouring. Every now and then I go to a bookshop in the centre of the city and I get an armful of reading matter: Montessori, Melanie Klein, and my favourite author Alexander Neill, founder of Summerhill School, who writes about the freedom I too plan to bestow in abundance upon my Petros.

Along with these, I'm also reading – late at night, so that Tassos won't see them and start worrying – books on depression and how it can be dealt with, because the germ of doubt has visited me quite a few times; I know that all this hyperactivity is in part a normal result of the natural alertness that any new mother feels, but when I spend one straight month getting barely two hours of sleep every night and I'm still pumped and capable to do a thousand things at once, I can't help remembering my adolescent oscillations, where the almost bionic euphoria was succeeded by equally dramatic plummets.

My fears notwithstanding, this time I'm all prepared for the depression and if it comes, it'll find me ready for battle.

Because back then, when I was fourteen, what did I have in life? The love of Agis, growing more distant by the day, and the affection of Zoë who had a million things to take care of.

Whereas now, I feel capable of facing anything.

(And yet, years later, I'll reminisce about those days and wonder *What has changed? Petros still fills up my life. So why do I feel so empty?* And all the books in the world won't be able to solve the mystery of my grief, or to console me.)

The Horrors of Others: Uncle Death

When Petros turns two and becomes a regular little beast running about and needing all kinds of attention, while at the same Tassos starts to show his displeasure at me (and justly so: not only do I ignore him completely, I've become the worst kind of housewife, too bored to pick up discarded clothes or even cook a decent meal not intended for a two-year-old), I realize I'm very close to a breakdown and I need help.

But my mother is seventy years old now and although she adores her grandson ("*The aristocrat of the family*" she calls him, because he's learnt how to answer her phone calls by saying, "Good morning, grandmother!", and when he eats he never gets messy like most kids his age), she didn't even like raising her own children – there's not a chance that she's going to help out with mine. Tassos's mother is equally if not more incapable of helping, and that stuffed-bird-look in her eyes because of all the medication she's taking creeps me out; it seems to me an example of what I might become if I'm not careful. (Careful of what? How?)

So I turn to the only person who is already at our place almost every day, to the only woman whose heart has love enough for everyone, even if she has never received herself one millionth of the love she deserves.

And when I ask her to come for a few hours every day to help out with the housework or look after Petros when I feel I'm about to fall apart and just lie down and stare at the ceiling for two hours straight, it's as if I've finally given her what life has deprived her of: a child of her own.

Because, as I've said before, Zoë's marriage has not turned out well.

At the age of thirty, she fell in love with Lazaros, a guy twenty years older than her, who dyed his hair auburn, and the way he used to dress up in floor-length shiny leather coats with more jewellery than Liberace in Vegas – there wasn't a single woman who'd see him coming and not make a run for it, lest he tried to steal her cold cream. But Zoë, being naïve and ever submissive, gave in to Lazaros's unimaginable charms, even though he treated her abominably from the start of their relationship: the bastard was kinder to Mama Rini and our washerwoman than to this wonderful woman who was stupid enough to fall in love with him.

For one thing, he indoctrinated her. In the years following the junta, he would drag her to all these Communist Party meetings, where they both stood out like sore thumbs: Zoë terrified by the bearded youths bellowing at one another, and Lazaros bedecked in fur coats with three rings per finger.

Also he forced her to sleep on a tiny, hard sofa, while he stretched his worthless hide on their double bed. I'll be damned if the poor woman ever received a tender husband's caress; Agis claims Zoë is still a virgin.

However, the worst thing about Lazaros is his pathological stinginess. Even though he's quite well off, living it up thanks to the apartments he owns and rents out, and despite the added income of a disability pension from his wartime service (though what this idiot did in the war, I can't imagine – unless they used him as their bitch), he's chosen as their home a pokey, sunless mezzanine apartment that reeks of mould from the peeling and rotting hundred-year-old wallpaper. It doesn't even have a boiler, so that in order for the piece of scum to enjoy his daily bath – a mandatory ritual, like the hair mask he slathers on his thinning hair, for which Zoë has to whisk together eggs, olive oil and honey – she is forced to boil water on the stove, pot after pot of it, and when it slightly cools off, douse him slowly with it while he sits on a plastic stool: he may be a Communist, but he has no qualms about taking advantage of his proletarian wife.

Gently at first and then furiously, I've tried a thousand times to make her realize the man is torturing her with his thriftiness and bitching and overall despotism.

Until one day I can't take it anymore, because the poor woman asks me for the umpteenth time if she can take a shower before leaving our place (as if I'd ever say no).

I start shouting at her: "How can you claim that man loves you when he won't even get you a boiler so you can wash your twat?"

And when she recovers from laughing, she says: "Shush! You don't know him, deep down Lazaros has a heart of gold."

"The only gold he has, he's wearing it," I reply, but she pays no attention. She even gives in to her hubby's latest obsession and lugs around all of his jewellery in two huge plastic bags – we're talking twenty pounds here – because he fears some burglar might break in and steal his tiaras. Which is insane, because if anyone actually did break into that hovel, they'd feel so sorry for the people who lived there they'd probably leave a handful of coins on the coffee table before taking off.

"You silly woman, are you out of your mind? Why doesn't he just rent a safety deposit box?" I say. This time I'm really pissed off; Zoë is my mother, and I won't stand watching her pant and gasp on the bus because she's carrying that revolting faggot's precious jewellery. But he won't hear of it, because the banks, he says, are bloodsuckers, an instrument of the ruling class. "Bullshit!" I cry. "*He*'s the one sucking *your* blood!"

But there's no changing Zoë's mind. Sometimes I honestly wonder if she's a masochist, if the violence and the humiliations she has suffered in her lifetime – from being left to die as a baby and being treated like a slave by her aunt, to the trials this sleazeball subjects her to – has left such an imprint on her soul that she can't feel joy unless she's suffering.

For instance, her endurance of pain is almost too extreme: she can take a casserole out of the oven without oven mittens, or grab a hard-boiled egg right out of the boiling water and peel it, especially if it's intended for Petros – because that's where Zoë's maternal love becomes truly pathological. She can carry him around in her arms for hours on end (although he weighs twenty-four pounds by now), until she pees her pants because the poor dear is slightly incontinent (which is why I get so mad with that asshole who's making her lug about all that weight every day!) and then she goes and hides in the bathroom to wash her underwear unnoticed with steaming-hot water and soap, rather than dirty our washing machine – something else that Lazaros hasn't got her, relegating her to the life of a 19th century washerwoman.

My Petros repays her worship in full. The second the intercom buzzes, he leaps up from whatever he's doing to wait in the hall – when he sees the elevator door open, he shouts: "Auntie Zoë!" and rushes into her embrace like a cannonball. Poor Tassos feels completely dethroned: not only does he slave all day at work to feed us, he comes home and finds his son in the midst of his own personal harem – for apart from Zoë, we're often visited by neighbour girls who can't get enough of pinching Petros's cheeks and making him sing them 'Frère Jacques'. His dad worries, naturally, that this exclusively female entourage may somehow affect his son's sexuality. But I am adamant: he has no reason to worry – he's only worried because his own brother is gay and he's afraid there might be some kind of predisposition in the family. I assure him that nothing of the sort has ever been proven scientifically and barely stop myself from adding, *Even if he grows up to be a lover of goats, he'll still be God's gift in my eyes.*

To get back to the subject of Zoë, his beloved auntie. When I doze off from exhaustion, he follows her around everywhere – even to the bathroom, where he watches her showering, astonished by her huge, drooping breasts. He points at them and shouts, "*Bell Boobies!*" It always cracks us up, even though Tassos thinks this, too, is a bit weird. "She's not his mother to see her naked," he remarks. I don't know, maybe he's right – but how can you hold back on love? Even in its maddest excess, love can't hurt. Can it?

As for his Uncle Lazaros, he doesn't even want to look at him. The few times he's been over to visit – usually to try and convince Tassos to give him a gold filling free of charge – despite all his fake cooing and smiling, Petros turns his back to him, grim as a grownup, goes to his room to play and doesn't set foot in the living room until Lazaros is gone. Perhaps he merely senses my own dislike for the man, yet I believe that, with that almost preternatural intuition children are capable of, he understands that Lazaros has a rotten soul.

(And years later, when I'll give in to his pleading and let him stay for a night at Zoë's place, he'll come back and say, "If auntie's name is Zoë" – which, in Greek, means *life* – "*he* ought to be called Death.")

And unfortunately, he's right. For Zoë has a bad heart, even though she's unaware of her condition, despite the constant headaches and the shortness of breath and her swollen fingertips – a sure sign that something is wrong, as Tassos says – and for all my pleading, she'll always refuse to see a cardiologist. "It's nothing, I'm just getting old." And when she dies suddenly at sixty-five, Lazaros, overcome with guilt, will confess that it was he who wouldn't let her go to a doctor, so that no other man would see her naked – even if that putrid man never gave her a single night of pleasure himself. And the foolish, kind-hearted woman obeyed his every whim till her last breath, enduring her heart's sickness the same way she endured the childlessness.

If there's one thing I regret about not ending up in Hell, is that I never had the pleasure of seeing Lazaros there, burning and burning for all eternity.

Journal d'amour

I have a secret.

At night, when the boys are sleeping, I shut myself in the

spare bedroom – Petros's room, as I try to think of it so I can get used to the unthinkable, that one day an entire wall is going to stand between us – and write my diary, which by now has added up to several volumes.

But I'm not writing about vague impressions and feelings; nor do I select the day's highest moments. No: what I do is record Petros's life minute by minute, memorizing, without knowing exactly how, the ever-eventful days – I, who couldn't memorize anything, now don't forget a single detail (what he ate, said, laughed at, what he looked like while he slept and I watched over him reverently) and hoard it avidly, because life goes by so swiftly, like water through my fingers, and I don't want to lose anything to the mists of memory: I want a written monument to remind me of everything that happened.

Naturally, the greatest part of the journal – page upon page of it – is dedicated to his growth and development.

For example, he learns to use the potty before he even turns two and a half and calls me when he's done to admire his good work.

The precious freedom suggested by the Summerhill School exhausts me and when I realize I'd like to curtail it a bit, it's already too late: Petros has found out he is free to draw on the walls whenever he feels like it (and afterwards Zoë and I spend hours scrubbing off today's works of art so he can draw on them again tomorrow), to toss all his toys off the balcony so as to make us run down and fetch them, or to barge in the living room and proudly exhibit his erection to anyone who happens to be there: friends, relatives, neighbours. Tassos is appalled by his behaviour and says we ought to spank him every now and then before he turns into a total brat, but the mere sound of the word (*My Petros, a brat?*) makes me want to slap him and shut his mouth so he'll stop saying such nonsense. "Did you like it when you got spanked as a kid?" I ask, "Because I didn't like it one bit." "I might have minded," he replies, "but look at me now – it didn't hurt me. I'm fine." Fine, yes – but not perfect. And Petros is – and must remain at all costs – perfect. Even though he wears me out with his idiosyncrasies and his obsessions.

Like the clothes thing. For instance, he's got one pair of denim dungarees that he loves so much, he refuses to dress in anything else; no matter how often I've tried, he just starts squealing: "I don't love you anymore!" and I'm terrified that my child is going to hate me, so I relent and dress him once again with his tattered and dirty dungarees. And he's so very clever, bless him: when I buy him a couple of pairs just like his favourite ones, he doesn't want them: the fabric is too coarse, their colour isn't faded enough, they aren't his dungarees. And every other night I wash the damn dungarees in the bathtub, so that the washing machine won't wake him up, and afterwards I spend hours ironing them to dry. I crumple and crease and sit on them, so he won't realize they've been cleaned while he slept.

Or his refusal to eat. I'm mad with worry that he's undernourished, that at three years of age he's not as tall as he ought to be (I know, because I keep measuring him and comparing the results with normal growth diagrams), but the only kind of dairy he'll touch is ice cream, be it summer or winter; he's capable of spending the whole day on just one ice cream stick, while I'm in a cold sweat that if he doesn't get his requisite daily calories, he'll get sick and die and then I'll die too.

I'm also terribly concerned about his aggressiveness. While we were summering in Halkidiki, in the village of Fourka, he had already shown destructive tendencies from the age of two – first by shattering a decorative gnome in the garden, because they were copies of the Disney Seven Dwarfs, and he couldn't stand Grumpy. So he grabbed a stone and smashed the thing to pieces. And if that weren't enough, he found an old, half-rotten power pole that had come loose as a result of a flood and kept pushing and yanking at it like a tiny Samson till it crashed to the ground – it was pure luck that he didn't get electrocuted. His father of course couldn't help but yell at him. Petros burst into tears and I said: "Tassos, that's enough. He's a child, he was just playing." But when our landlady dared express her views on the subject, informing us that the kid had psychological issues, all hell broke loose: I grabbed her hair and smashed her face into the wall. Luckily Tassos managed to pull us apart before I killed the bitch who had the nerve to badmouth my son. Needless to say we didn't set foot in that village again: we're still wanted there.

And this year, at the seaside village of Ouranoupolis, he takes an unexpected, dramatic revenge on his four-year-old cousin Minas Agis's older son – who is a year and a half older that him and roughhouses him as kids that age are prone to do to younger toddlers: dunking his head into the sea, tossing his ice cream into the sand, kicking the sand castles he's just built… I watch all this, smoking and grinding my teeth so as not to leap up and thrash the fucking little bully who's tormenting my Petros; he's my nephew, so I try to grin and bear it, because otherwise the two of them are the best of friends. One evening, however, while we're sitting at the beach, drinking beer and reminiscing with Agis about the various antics of the Horianos family, near-tragedy strikes: Minas has just pushed his little cousin into the sea fully clothed, and now is sitting and innocently tearing up weeds from the sand, when Petros finds a broken Coke bottle lying around and smashes it on Minas's head, opening a wound that starts bleeding like a fountain. Minas howls with pain, his mother howls with terror, we're pretty much all howling, while

Tassos, the most sober of the group, grabs the boy and rushes him off to the nearest hospital to get the wound sutured. And all the while Petros gazes at us with a half-grin peculiar for a child so small. I know what Agis and his wife Ritsa are thinking: it's only natural that the loony mother would produce a loony son. Two years will pass until we vacation together again.

But even more of the journal's pages are dedicated to Petros's accomplishments: the facility with which he learns to read and write both Greek and French. Soon enough we're able to have whole conversations entirely in French, especially if we're keeping some secret from his father. Or his astonishing musical ear: he learns at once by heart every song he listens to and is able to sing it without even mashing up the lyrics (even if he doesn't comprehend what they're saying) like a tiny jukebox. I can't stop kissing him when he sings! No matter how carefully I memorize them, there's no counting our kisses and embraces.

Lastly, written in red ink (in order to stand out on the page, so that hopefully I won't repeat them), the journal recounts my own crimes, big and small – which I wish I hadn't committed, but something within me (love, hopefully) blinds me many times.

The vomiting thing, for instance. A little before he turns two, one evening as we're driving back home from Peraia, we stop at a kiosk to get cigarettes and Petros asks for a chocolate muffin. I stupidly fail to check the expiration date on the damn thing and by the time we're home he's already gobbled it up – and when I do look at the packaging, I realize it expired a week ago. Despite Tassos's insistence that the child will be fine, the worst-case scenario being that he gets the runs, I panic, force him to drive us to the hospital and talk the doctor into giving Petros an emetic – so the poor kid starts throwing up convulsively until he all but faints. From that night onwards, my son will develop a pathological terror of vomiting, preferring to spend two days with an upset stomach from a bug or a flu than relive the horrible experience of that long-ago night.

Or the shameful fact that I systematically monopolize his time, luring him away from other kids with books, board games, presents and sweets, any sort of overindulgence so he won't go away and leave the house as empty as my heart – for what if the other boys start throwing stones at one another and Petros loses an eye? I'd sooner gouge both my own eyes out with a spoon! So we end up spending day after day just the two of us, watching movies on video, singing songs, and having a great time all in all. However, this attachment to me that I'm so diligently cultivating will make my son socially maladaptive: all through his childhood until his high-school years, he'll hesitate to take the first step that building a friendship often requires, because he won't know how it's done, since other kids don't love him unconditionally like his mother does, nor comply to his every whim. Like Nikos Tsiforos, one of my favourite writers, says, *It was all the fairy tales that finally got Little Red Riding Hood.* And I'm simply hoping that the books will somehow save him in the end.

But the gravest crime, which I'll live to regret, is on his fifth birthday, when estimating that the only things he's eaten all day are a couple of Mars bars and a cup of orange juice, I go to the nearest pharmacy and get a bottle of appetite stimulant called Mosegor, and start giving him a spoonful each day along with royal jelly, until my Petros balloons to double his weight within a matter of months. He'll be chubby for the remainder of his childhood; it will take him more than fifteen years to shed this weight I put on him like a curse.

Petros will find those diaries (eight volumes in total,

chronicling the first eight years of his life in every detail) stashed away in the back of a wardrobe, several years after I'm gone.

He'll keep them. But he'll never read them.

The Ceremony of Goodbyes

And then comes the trial of school.

Of nursery school, that is, because I didn't send him to preschool – he was just a baby; he was barely potty-trained (or so I told myself). It is a posh place up in the mountainous suburb of Panorama and the bus will be taking him away from me at seven in the morning and bring him back at two: seven hours of desolation. I dread to think how I'm supposed to fill them.

The last few days before the school opens, while Petros is ecstatic about the whole idea and with all his new belongings – the red satchel with the STOP sign on the back, the pencil case, the drawing pad and the card with his name which he'll be wearing on his lapel (Why, though? Surely they'll be able to tell my kid apart?) – I sneak away and take half or sometimes a whole Valium from the stash Dr Lemonis, the Horianos family shrink, has prescribed for my nerves, washing it down with a beer: it's the only way I can calm down. I don't care if Tassos is frowning at me, saying the boy will be upset and get scared. I'd rather be a little hazy if the alternative is that Petros sees me shaking or bursting into tears.

But when the first day arrives, I'm at the end of my tether.

Because when the school bus arrives and Petros realizes he'll have to get on it on his own, without his mum, and go to a strange place called nursery school where he won't know a soul, he starts weeping and falls into my arms begging to stay with me or that I'll go along. Fortunately, the books I've read have prepared me for just this sort of reaction. Smiling yet determined, I kneel down, wipe away his tears and promise him that the hours will fly away, that he'll meet a ton of new friends and play all sorts of games, and he'll be back home before he knows it and I'll have made him his favourite chocolate custard. I reassure him that his mother adores him and that I'll be thinking of him the whole time so it will really be as if we're still together.

I'm wasting my breath, though. With his stooped shoulders shaking uncontrollably, Petros, my angel, boards the bus and, before the lady who accompanies the children can catch him, runs all the way to the back, climbs on the seats and, pressing his tear-streaked little face into the rear window, starts banging his fists and screaming: "Mum! Mum!", while the school bus drives away, tearing out my heart.

I feel defenceless, unable to endure more. I feel like a crushed worm, like a dead person who oddly stands upright.

So I drag myself back home, ask Zoë to take care of the cooking and the housework – especially the chocolate custard I've promised him – and then I go to the bathroom and take my first-ever overdose: two Valiums and two beers downed in quick succession.

Tassos will rouse me at one, having rushed home from the hospital when Zoë called and told him she couldn't wake me up. He will drag me to the bathroom, cursing and yelling at me to make myself presentable – Petros can't come home on his first day of school and find his mother all wild-haired and spaced-out.

After two cups of strong coffee I somewhat recover and prepare the custard myself – sprinkling it with icing sugar just the way he likes it – and when the door opens and he comes back to me, my heart is brimming over with childish glee.

Talking nonstop, he recounts the games and the crafts and

everything he's been up to, reeling off first names and last names, while I smile broadly and hope he doesn't realize that I'd like to set fire to his school, to every school in the world.

And from the next day onward, the same thing happens with minor variations: sometimes I manage to wake up in time, some days Petros comes home and finds me sleeping and Zoë tells him I got tired from all the cooking and the house chores and takes him for a walk, while on other days I stay up and am relatively active with just half a Valium and no booze, because he's developed a keen nose for beer, dislikes its bitter tang and says: "Mummy, you stink."

I wish that it would never end, that first day with its unbridled enthusiasm, even if I was a total mess.

But sadly, day after day and week after week, Petros, who knows me better than anyone, realizes that something's wrong with me and it's the school's fault. So he starts acting up. One day he wets himself, although he's been potty-trained for years, another day he trashes his classroom and finally, out of the blue, he attacks his classmate, Harry (a reserved, slothful and submissive kid who until then was his friend, or at least the agreeing party to all the games Petros devised) and beats him up until he bloodies the poor boy's nose. The parents are called in and we drive up to Panorama beside ourselves with worry (I've even recovered from the couple of Valiums I've taken, because I haven't understood which kid beat up which and I'm scared out of my wits). I find Harry's father, who is divorced and the father of two older children, has cornered a terrified Petros and, raising his fist, threatened that if he lays a finger on his son ever again, he'll give him the beating of his life.

(I'd rather not remember what happened next, but I do – as if all that I thought had been erased by dying now appears before me, etched in marble. The outcome was that Harry's father took his son to some other school, after ending up minus a handful of bloody hair torn out of his head).

All this – my sickness which gains ground day after day, Petros's often uncontrollable behaviour and Tassos's displeasure which hurts more than I expected – I'll try to cure, giving my son the greatest gift in my powers.

Something which I dream might save me as well, temper my pathological fixation to my son and give me another five or six years of love and happiness and healthy maternal attachment.

But it'll be the wrong year.

The wrong life.

Solo

And what about Tassos? What goes on in his mind and in his heart all these years?

It can't have been easy watching his wife, whom he once fell in love with, stricken by a disease similar to the one that crippled his own mother, a disease he never learned to handle without being crushed.

It can't have been easy feeling this same woman – his mentally ill wife, whom he thought he'd be able to cure with his love – grow cold and distant towards him from the moment his son was born, focusing all her passion on the one man he himself created and thus cannot compete with.

Nor has it been easy working ceaselessly all day without ever receiving a kind word like the hundreds lavished on his son, because the woman he once fell in love with has abandoned him forever, even if she shares the same cold, unhappy bed while he sleeps.

And although I am a riddle which over time he'll learn to accept as hopeless and unsolvable, Petros is a riddle he can't afford to ignore – and yet how can you ever win over a heart that is already given elsewhere, a child who sees and knows so little of you, who talks in a language you don't even know right in your face, while conspiring with a mother who overwhelms every aspect of his life? Poor Tassos (no more endearments from me, no more caresses) isn't accustomed to effusive shows of emotion: his father was always a cold and distant man and his mother's sweetness was forever lost behind the ashen veil of her psychosis, so he has no way of knowing how to express his immense love with words, gestures and caresses. Even his praises of Petros are brief as sneezes, because he feels (or, rather, thinks) that his son is getting enough of those and doesn't need them. (Sadly, he's mistaken – Petros needs his praise even more than he does mine.) So he does the only thing he can: he takes pictures. No child apart from Hollywood child actors has ever been as obsessively photographed as Petros: dozens and hundreds of films, cupboards bursting with photos and negatives, and albums, so many albums we're eventually forced to give away blankets and clothes so we can accommodate the papery immortality they contain.

My husband, not knowing whether I love him anymore because I never say so or show it in any way, will try desperately to win his son's attention during the weekends, the only free time he has. However, he'll find out that his interests leave Petros cold and the boy would rather spend the weekends like any other day, glued to his mother, of whom he is deprived while at school – and when he consents to his father's suggestions out of a sense of obligation, or because his Mum talked him into it, he'll be glum and despondent, as if he's already rejected him and everything he wishes to share with him.

So Tassos will turn to the only child left to him: the one that, at the age of thirty, he still carries secretly within, bursting with the vigour of all neglected children.

He will cultivate interests and passions both elaborate and time-consuming to fill the empty hours when no one at home seems to want him around. He'll become a member of the CB Radio Club and spend endless hours speaking to other lonely men like him, husbands and fathers who are also seeking what they can't find at home: company, more than anything else. He'll also enrol at the Thessaloniki Aero Club and learn how to fly a small plane, studying everything from aerodynamics and aerospace engineering to meteorology, and he'll do all the necessary training to get his licence and become an incredible pilot, as if he were born for it – flying light aircrafts like the ones he dreamt of as a boy. On his first solo flight, from his phone call before takeoff to the phone call after landing, I will spend the whole time shut in the bedroom, praying on my knees to Saint Nectarios to keep my Tassos safe. (However, when the time comes and I see the glow of adventure-craving in Petros's eyes, I'll swallow all my fears and give him my blessing to go for a ride in his father's plane – and so, from the age of six, Petros will be flying with his father as a pilot all around Thessaloniki, to the islands and also to faraway places like Rome and Florence.)

Another common passion that Tassos shares with his son is their fascination with computers. Because – and I apologize it took me so long to mention this – Tassos is the most generous, extravagant husband in the whole wide world; when it's about giving joy by spending money, he doesn't think twice about it, even if he has to work thirteen-hour days at the hospital and his practice. So my Petros is going to have his own personal computer from the age of five: first a Commodore 64, which is succeeded by an Amstrad 6128, then a Commodore Amiga, and so on. (I know all this terrible stuff because I spend hours and days watching Petros play his various games, and get roaring mad whenever he loses; then he regales me with tales from what he calls his 'adventures', like novels with the player as protagonist, which I condone wholeheartedly because they're doing wonders for his English vocabulary.)

Of course, as is to be expected when two people grow so rapidly and dramatically apart, there's some inevitable tension between Tassos and me – especially since I'm struggling with a yet-undiagnosed case of bipolar disorder, which makes me prone to outbursts and quarrels and tears and scenes and all kinds of petty punishments.

For at night, when Petros is asleep, I become a woman all over again and I worry when my husband hasn't come home yet. And if he happens to be at the Aero Club till late, I call him and let him have it, and then start shouting at him the moment he steps in, not caring that my son, roused by my yelling, hides behind the door shaking like a leaf. I become jealous, malicious; although I rarely give myself to Tassos, and only after he's begged for it – and even then, far from eagerly – I imagine his body entwined with the bodies of dozens of other women, younger and thinner than me, who acknowledge how loveable he is and throw themselves at him without a moment's thought. These women, for the time being at least, exist solely in my imagination, but their ghosts haunt my sleepless nights: those hours when I can, with just one touch, bridge the chasm, but stubbornly refuse to, wanting Tassos to share my sleeplessness and misery. And when he falls asleep from exhaustion, I get out of bed and, tiptoeing about, I sniff at his clothes like a hound, go through his pockets and his briefcase – in the end, weary and frazzled like a not-so-live wire, I throw myself on the sofa with my headphones on and let the music carry me away to dreams, or fits of sobbing, or to the place where the tender and loving man I think I deserve lives, a man with the heart of Petros and the shape of Tassos, to whom I'm mother in the morning and wife at night.

And the real-life, ignored Tassos dreams his own dreams, equally elusive, unsuspecting of the twenty years of hell awaiting him.

The Horrors of Others: My Nephews and Nieces

I loved my siblings' children from the moment I saw them, as if their blood called to me. They'd say, "Auntie Katerina," and their little faces would light up.

However, my siblings never showed the same love toward my own son – quite the opposite.

The morning of my death, while Petros is struggling to deal with the coroner, the police and the undertaker – as well as with the thought that the woman who gave him life just threw her own away – he will call both my brothers and my sister, but to no avail. Despite their sobbing and hysterics, none of them nor any of their spouses will come to the aid of their nephew, who has just shouldered such an enormous cross without any siblings to share the horror and the pain with, and whose father, in a stroke of bad luck, is away in Athens at a conference. During the following year, the horrible year when my boys will be all alone, fighting continuously in hope of forgetting their grief, not only will the Horianos children never, not once, set foot in the apartment where they spent so many holidays and family gatherings, but they won't even call, as if they're terrified their dead sister might pick up the phone.

Though I couldn't care less about their betrayal of me, which

I sampled enough times in the past, I do care and in fact am full of white-hot anger that they turned their backs on my son when he needed them most.

The proof: for years to come, none of them will be able to look Petros in the eye.

And I don't give a shit about their ludicrous excuses, or whether my suicide filled them with such guilt they couldn't bear to be in my home anymore, or dial its phone number. If Tassos and Petros managed to grapple with their own infinitely greater guilt, then surely they could drop by – even if drugged up to the eyeballs – just once, on his birthday for instance, just to see how their bereaved nephew was coping.

And if you're wondering what sort of people would behave like that, I'll tell you.

For many times my siblings showed in their tacit way – as well as actually saying it to my face – that they considered me unfit as a mother, because my illness did irreparable damage to Petros, and believed he ought to be taken away from me so he could grow up in a calm and loving environment.

Loving, huh? Well, see for yourselves.

What sort of parent grabs their child's hand and presses it onto the burning stove just because the kid's making a racket and annoying them?

What sort of parent throws their six-month-old baby to the floor because it woke them up with its crying, shattering its still-half-formed leg?

What sort of parent ties their kids to their beds because it's still early and they don't want to go to sleep?

What sort of parent, without suffering the slightest financial hardship, abandons their child to the exclusive care of its grandparents, and only sees it again when it's four years old and doesn't recognize them anymore?

What sort of parent leaves their kids unbathed for so long that the school nurse sends them a note saying they should take the little ones to a dermatologist? (Who, rubbing the brown spots of on their tiny hands with a little cotton and rubbing alcohol, discovers only a criminal lack of washing?)

What sort of parent – in the year 1987 – would encourage their child to give up school to do something more practical?

These are the lives and works of the Horianos siblings.

But they said I was the mad one, the sick one, the unsuitable one…

In the Shadow of the Dead: Mama Rini

My mother was never well.

Aside from the consumption that afflicted her in her youth, leaving her for the rest of her life with breathlessness and a hoarse voice, the six times she got pregnant in the course of fifteen years will drain the calcium from her bones, causing her a severe osteoporosis, as well as doing such grave damage to her bladder and her womb that by the age of sixty she's already incontinent and suffers from womb prolapse and the indignity of adult diapers. As for her teeth, from the age of fifty to her death at seventy-two, she'll go through five different sets of dentures – the last two or three courtesy of her beloved son-in-law Tassos who will act as her primary personal physician. Even when he insists that she should consult a specialist, Mama Rini won't hear of it: "Only you know me well enough," she says, "for you're my doctor, body and soul." (Agis always claimed that Mum had a crush on Tassos, and he was probably right.) I will always remember how this woman, shy to the point of prudishness towards her husband and children, would pull off her clothes in rapid succession when about to be examined by Tassos, baring her huge white buttocks for a shot, or indeed her breasts (the sanctum sanctorum of her body that even Dad wasn't allowed to see with the lights on, because of the scar left by the resection of her tuberculoid lung), eagerly awaiting the touch of his stethoscope.

Despite Tassos's care and prescriptions, during the last few years Mum's health steadily declines: her high blood sugar, which she neglects like all elderly people with a sweet tooth, has damaged her eyesight; her shortness of breath often becomes so severe that she needs additional oxygenation; an obstinate case of erysipelas makes both her arms itchy as hell; and finally, her bones begin to shatter at the slightest touch, even in her sleep (*pathological fractures*, Tassos calls them), so that every now and then poor Mama Rini lies supine in some hospital, limb in a cast, forced to breathe the same air as people she thought she'd left forever behind when she married Minas and moved out of the shack. (The most unforgettable incident is having to spend a night in the same room with an old lady who takes pride in the fact that her body has never been touched by water, so as not to wash away the myrrh with which she was anointed at her christening.)

Thus, almost deaf and half-blind, with her feet swollen by phlebitis, she'll barely make it to May 1985, whereupon she'll predict – in an unprecedented moment of resignation – that her birthday on the 25th will find her in the afterlife; a prophecy that will be fulfilled with the chilling accuracy of coincidence.

Yet two nights before her last, bed-ridden after a bout of bronchitis and wearing an oxygen mask, she'll call and ask me to go and see her, because there's something she needs to confide in me, she says, so she can die in peace.

Thinking like all children that my parents are immortal, I

ignore the drama and hyperbole and visit her more out of curiosity – partly because Mama Rini was never the confiding type, and partly because one would expect her to grant this special honour to her firstborn, her beloved Myron.

But I am mistaken in what I'm expecting to hear. I've just shut the boudoir doors behind me as she ordered me to do (Dad had always a hellishly acute sense of hearing, and even now, at eighty-four, he can pick up the faintest spoken word like a wolf listening to the movements of its prey), and I'm sure Mum will tell me something that has to do with her will (since we all know that, being superstitious, she has never drawn one). However, she grabs me by the wrist and makes me swear never to repeat what she's about to tell me, not even to my siblings and especially not to my father. "If he finds out, my girl, that I've been keeping a secret like this from him, he's fully capable of coming to my grave every day to shit on it."

My curiosity reaches a peak – judging by her desperate tone and her wild eyes, I've started to imagine youthful, illicit love affairs, or even that one of her children wasn't fathered by Papa Minas but by some bygone flame – so when she merely reveals that her mother was Jewish and was forced to convert to Christianity and have her name changed in order to marry my grandfather (my attention is already wandering, for I truly believe my mother is going senile with all this talk about Jewish ancestors), I get a powerful feeling of anticlimax. You see, I'm thoroughly ignorant of the blood rules governing nomadic tribes, whose female populations were repeatedly raped and had to protect their lineage, so I think to myself, *Great. So grandma was a Jew, and we are one fourth Jewish – apart from Anatolian, Vlach, and redneck.* Talk about a letdown.

And when two days later Mama Rini dies in her sleep from pulmonary edema, I keep her secret, like I promised, because I view it as the delirium of a dying soul, dreaming up hidden sins, and also because my brothers and I are far more devastated than we expected. The death of our mother, of that unloving, cold woman whom we'd never let into our hearts, will nonetheless cripple us so savagely that none of us will have the courage to go to our childhood home and comfort our old, widowed, desolate father, or even go to her funeral the next day. (The burden will be borne once more by our spouses, same as in the past, and so it will be in the future.)

As to my mother's deathbed confession, I'll recall it many years later, after the death of her neighbour and close friend, an elderly Jewish lady who also shared her story with me, one infinitely more barbaric. However, when I dare to hint at the matter in front of my siblings, their reaction will be worse than Mama Rini imagined her husband's to be. They'll say I'm lying, that the whole thing is one of my hallucinations and in the end they too will make me swear never to speak a word of this to anyone, in case this '*stigma*' affects their families and children.

Yet despite all my vows, I shall reveal the truth to my son.

I'm sorry, Mum. If you were so ashamed of it, you should have taken it to your grave.

The Wrong Thighs

Three weeks have passed since the death of my mother, and I daresay I'm almost well enough. I can handle the fact that Petros, a first-grader now, is away at school for seven hours a day, thanks to my new wonder drug: three tablets a day of an antidepressant called Minitran which contains a slight dose of sedative. Dr Lemonis has also prescribed some Valium, but he's made me promise that I'll only take one when I'm in a really bad state, if I can't sleep for instance or if I feel a panic attack coming on. You can't eat benzos like sweets, he says, because you develop a tolerance to them and then you have to up the dosage for them to work. Are we clear? Of course. Absolutely. I'll be as obedient as Adam and Eve.

Zoë is a huge help, an invaluable asset; without her I wouldn't make it. For one thing, it's as if I've got my mother – a *real, proper* mother – with me every single day. On the other hand, in order for Petros to live in as normal as possible a home, she drills me whenever I'm brooding too much, so that I can function properly as a housewife and mother: cook, clean, and take care of myself ("You don't want the poor boy to see you looking like a madwoman and freak him out"). And, it goes without saying, not a drop of alcohol.

The help I most desperately need is, of course, the one I refuse to consider, though it has been offered many times. Quite recently, a friend of Myron's, a psychoanalyst who studied in Paris and has returned to his native Thessaloniki, has repeatedly asked me if I'd like to '*work through some issues with him*' – that is, lie down on his couch and be analyzed. But I don't want to dredge up old traumas, nor do I care about the causes or the origin of my disease. You cannot change the past; what is important is the present. (Plus, I'm scared. There's no guarantee that I won't stumble upon some huge repressed trauma and get in an even worse mess.) Oh no: mum's the word, just try and focus on the present, on the life you've got ahead of you. Unfortunately, I'll stick to this naïve, self-destructive opinion of psychotherapy – which I'm in such dire need of – till the very end.

So I fill up my under-occupied mind and my empty Petros-less hours with as much of Petros as possible: his accomplishments at school, his amazing facility in foreign languages (he's had just one year of English and he's already practically fluent), his astonishing musical ear (he can play on his keyboard whatever song we ask of him, even though he's never had a single piano lesson!) and his oh-so-promising future, which I can daydream about for hours on end, as if it's going to be my own. I fancy him a university professor, a prime minister, a Nobel laureate, a multiple-page entry in every encyclopaedia. And meanwhile I try to feed his insatiable mind however I can: with music, films, books, my own obsessions which Tassos finds a bit too adult. And every time he comes back from school with words of praise and gold stars on his homework and quizzes, every time his teacher speaks admiringly of him to the whole class, I feel myself growing taller, reaching as high as the clouds. I'm only troubled by his excess weight, combined with his denial to try any sport (which is my fault, because instead of making him go and kick a football with the neighbours' kids, I kept playing board games with him), but I trust that over the years he'll shed the weight. It's nothing critical anyway, he's just a little pudgy, which in any case makes him even more adorable.

So I'm very surprised when one afternoon, while Zoë is out washing the balcony, he takes me aside and says in a low voice that there's something he needs to talk to me about. There's only one thing that instantly comes to my mind: that he got into an argument with a classmate and used bad language. For Petros has developed a foul mouth beyond his years and the teacher often takes him to the principal, even though there are never any repercussions: Tassos has made sure they're aware that the boy's mother needs locking up (I'm perfectly okay with him saying that if it gets Petros off detention), so they never punish him. After all, the poor kid's just repeating what he hears at home – he's not possessed or anything, curses don't come to him out of the ether.

But when he keeps staring at the floor, silent and glum, and I ask him if he said any bad words in class, he shakes his head and looks as if he's in pain. By now I'm getting seriously worried. What's wrong with him?

"You know, Mum," he begins and falls silent.

"What is it, my little dove? Tell mama. I won't get angry no matter what it is."

"When you like something, but…" and he pauses again.

I wonder, does he enjoy killing stray cats and dogs? There was a kid in the neighbourhood, back when I was little, who used to lure strays to the entrance of his building and poison them. I honestly hope it's not —

And then, suddenly, realizing there's no sense beating around the bush, he blurts it out:

"I like So-and-So's thighs," he says, naming a boy in his class.

Up until a moment ago, I thought I was prepared for a revelation like this. I've read a ton of relevant articles and books. I know all about the fluid sexuality of children, about the negative Oedipus complex I may have caused by dethroning his father as a role model and surrounding him with women who adore him, women like Zoë and me, who render the conquest of another woman unnecessary. And I firmly believe – or rather I thought I did, up till a second ago – that I could deal with the dreaded issue, if and when it arose, with sobriety, calm and tenderness.

But now, as the seconds tick by and I'm lost for words, my initial urge is not to grab my son and hold him tight and assure him that everything's okay, that he's done nothing wrong and that I'll go on loving him as much as before and even more, whether this thing he feels changes or not. No, what I'd really like to do is swallow ten Valiums, wash them down with beer and sleep for three days straight so I don't have to think about the criminal mistakes I made, causing my son to become a homosexual (such a terrible word, I can't bear to even utter it in thought).

So much for my dreams of a glorious future for him; gone is the image of my son as a statesman, a famous writer or even a father of my grandchildren. In his forties he won't be found in encyclopaedias, but lurking around in the parks, cruising. Loneliness, scorn and squalor will swallow him up. He might even end up slain like Pasolini.

But the more Petros waits for an answer from me, the more heartbroken he seems – his chin is nearly touching his chest, his eyes brim with unshed tears. I have to say something, anything, I have to bite back my panic and smile.

So I hold him tight and say it's okay, these things happen, it might change over the years but even if it doesn't, there's nothing wrong with him, he's not a bad boy, he's my treasure just as he was and always will be, and I'll adore him more and more with every passing second. And yet, he still whispers: "I'm sorry" into my bosom.

The mere fact that he was ashamed to tell me and, even worse, the fact that he feels the need to apologize is proof that we live in a disgusting, rotten world.

But I'm a rotten and disgusting part of it myself.

Because as soon as he looks up and a hesitant smile blooms across his features, I take him gently by the shoulders, and with the conspiratorial look that I have when we're secretly making some dessert for just the two of us so that his dad won't complain that I'm making him fat, I tell him:

"But let's not tell Dad about it yet, all right?"

Another miserable silence. As if the one that's been eating me up weren't enough.

I had to drag my son into it and make him my accomplice.

In the Shadow of the Dead: Zoë

The autumn of 1985 will find me six months pregnant. How did that happen and why? Didn't I always feel that I'd never be able to love another child as much as Petros, ignoring both my husband's and my son's pleadings? Wasn't I terrified that if depression struck while I was raising one kid and carrying another, not even God Himself – let alone pills and Zoë – would be able to save me? What has changed then? How did I take such a momentous decision?

I did it partly for Petros. When his best friend Thodoris acquired a new sister, his beseeching became so intense and the stories he made up so elaborate – how he'd teach his little sister to swim and ride a bike and so many other things – that he broke my heart. How could I deny him the gift of a sibling when Tassos assured me that financially we could afford even two more kids, and insisted, justly in my opinion, that a second child would help me sever the umbilical cord that kept me dependent on Petros and which was rapidly becoming pathological?

But, to be honest, I did it more for me, figuring that another child would grant me six more years of coexistence (if not symbiosis), during the unthinkable, harrowing years when Petros would be away from home studying, working, falling and being in love. And that last thing weighed upon me terribly: the fact that, if he was and kept on being what I dreaded to even name because I was overwhelmed by remorse and despair and felt I'd been a failure as a mother, the outcome might not be the one I expected. He'd still be perfect and loveable as an angel, but only in my eyes – certainly not in the eyes of his father, or those of the world at large. (Being a despicable egoist, I even regretted the fact that I would never have grandchildren).

So now I sit and blissfully stroke my belly, accepting congratulations and wishes from all over. Petros touches my distended flesh diffidently to see if the baby's kicking and Tassos gazes at me with the adoration that has been absent from his eyes for years, hoping as I do that our baby daughter will change me for the better.

We know the baby's sex because my gynaecologist, judging that I shouldn't go off my medication during the first trimester at least, recently performed an amniocentesis and we found out I'm expecting a girl. We've even picked out a name: we're going to call her Zoë, even though at first Tassos objected, wanting to name his daughter after his mother. In the end, though, knowing what a tough year it's been for me and acknowledging Zoë's inestimable dedication to our family's happiness, he relented.

When Petros is at home, I make sure I devote my every moment to him, so he won't feel that the new baby is stealing me away from him and hate it, but when he's away at school I weave the most wonderful dreams about my beloved little Zoë, realizing to my astonishment that I adore her almost as much as I do Petros. Who knows, perhaps after she's born and I hold her in my arms and find myself once more in that distant paradise, the scales of my heart will balance as they should.

All this lasts until the accursed morning of my next scheduled amnio, when my doctor tells me he's not too thrilled about the baby's motility and heartbeat. He'd like me to stop taking my pills during the last trimester – something which my shrink also consents to, promising that even if I get depressed or have a panic attack (none of which has happened to me recently anyway), there are other ways to deal with it, like valerian infusions and passiflorine tablets and I don't know what else.

But I'm not listening. I've had six wonderful months, six months of not thinking once about depression, and I'm not about to sacrifice my hard-won happiness because that crook of a doctor frets for no reason. So I tell him I'm not going off my medication, end of discussion.

"Do you want the child to be born with some congenital problem and have to care of it for the rest of your life?" he says. "Some malformation or heart condition or God knows what else?"

He should know better than to terrorize a woman with my medical history; he should sweet-talk me into it, explain the potential dangers calmly and suggest that I try a few days without my meds first, then see if I can hold off taking them for another couple of months. If his approach had been that delicate, I might have gone with it.

But as it is, I'm both terrified (thinking up horrendous cases of teratogenesis) and incensed with the fucking quack, who six months earlier assured me that my dosage is low and harmless and now scares me to death using my own baby as a weapon.

"Fuck off, you son of a whore," I spit at him and leave his office in a hurry, with the laces of my pregnancy shoes undone.

Tassos catches up with me on the stairwell (for some reason I'm suddenly afraid to use the elevator), stops me and, kneeling before me, ties my shoelaces. "If you want my opinion –" he ventures.

"I do not. You just stick to your patients' teeth and your stupid tiny airplanes," I retort and hurry down the stairs seething with rage and barely-contained panic.

As soon as we're home, I go to the kitchen and fill up a tumbler with vodka. Tassos snatches it away and empties it into the sink. I slap his face – and then fall into his arms and start sobbing.

"Everything will be fine, my Katerina," he says. "You'll manage wonderfully even without the pills, as you've managed all these years. After all, you are such a terrific mother, everyone sings your praises about the wonders you've done with Petros."

Wiping away the tears and the snot, I give in on one condition: that I can take one last Valium to fall asleep – it's still eleven in the morning, and Zoë won't be coming before two because she has to take some of Lazaros's clothes to be altered by a tailor somewhere, and I want to feel better by then, so my boy doesn't come home to find me weeping and shaking like a leaf.

Tassos consents to one pill and then puts me to bed – and the moment I start snoring, he leaves for the hospital, where he's expected by people with pressing dental problems.

He shouldn't have left, you might say. Or he should have called someone –even my sister, who was an idle housewife like myself – and asked them to come over and keep an eye on me until Zoë arrived.

But he didn't know, he could never have imagined the outcome. I couldn't have imagined it either, if you'd asked me just one day before. It's something totally unthinkable, that's why it is veiled in such secrecy and anathema.

Half hour after falling asleep I suddenly sit up, drenched in sweat, my heart hammering away. Black thoughts flutter in my mind: a baby with a face like a Cubist portrait, eyes and nose all skewed-up and monstrous, a baby with a heart condition or Down's syndrome or with its spinal cord exposed, like a kitten I'd once seen behind a dumpster, left there by its mother to perish. How will I ever manage to raise a kid who is malformed, sick, or mentally challenged without succumbing to depression or going mad from guilt? No baby deserves a life like that, nor a mother like me, the same way I don't deserve a son like Petros, whom I've already damaged irreparably with my diseased love.

Perhaps all the Horianos children are carriers of some bad

gene, I think as I traipse over to the kitchen, where I empty out all the pills I have left, enough for two or three weeks or even a full month, and down them with the rest of the vodka. I don't know whether I want to die or to simply sleep without any dreams; anything to make this choking terror go away, so I won't have to think about anything anymore.

Two hours later, coming home early from the hospital because he has a bad feeling, Tassos finds me face-down on the bedroom floor in a semi-comatose state. As he will find out shortly after, the foetus has died – the overdose caused its tiny heart to stop, even though my own black heart managed to survive.

Our daughter Zoë is dead: her life-giving name wasn't enough to protect her from her mother's madness.

And since the doctors are forced to cut the baby into pieces to remove it, my womb will suffer such grave damage I'll never be able to conceive again.

This murder, the murder of my unborn daughter, will haunt me to the very end.

It will be my daily executioner.

Kicked and Caressed

By the time the hospital releases me, I'm so pumped up with antipsychotics that there's no way I'm going to be able to return to our place and manage any kind of tasks – not even with Zoë's help.

So once again we move back to my childhood home, where my father, despite his eighty-four years and incipient senility that manifested itself after Mum's death, will become Petros's guardian angel during the hours Tassos is away at work. He won't even let poor Zoë (*'that redneck servant girl'*) rob him of a single precious moment with his beloved grandson.

Tassos, watching him in the afternoon when Petros takes his after-lunch nap, speaks of a transformation: while the boy is at school, Papa Minas may sit for hours staring at one of Mum's wigs, silent and unresponsive or making sad, creepy comments like: "She went away and forgot to take her hair with her." Yet whenever the child is with him, it's as if he's shed forty years in a heartbeat: he makes his breakfast, takes him to the school bus stop, cooks lunch (this man who couldn't boil water is suddenly capable of making omelettes and steaks and even decent spaghetti and meatballs), helps Petros with his homework, watches TV with him, and in the evening, after Tassos kisses him goodnight, he sits on his bedside and, in a soft and warm paternal voice that I never had the privilege of enjoying as a child, recounts stories of the good old days: the same self-aggrandizing tales he used to tell us in order to impress us with his brilliance as a rich, self-made man, he now turns into wonderful fairy tales for the sake of Petros.

Of course, I'll only find out about all this later. I'm spending those same days and nights in a sleeping bag on the floor of my old room, because my sleep is so restless I kept falling off the bed. I feed myself pistachios, one to two bottles of ouzo per day, and the marvellous new cocktail prescribed by Dr Lemonis: Largactil, Akineton, Depamide and Rohypnol. I sleep all the time to stop myself from contemplating the crime I've committed, to stop feeling the urge to kill myself, but my accursed brain seems to be getting more than enough sleep and I spend most of my torturous hours in a groggy daze, feeling and not-feeling, aware and unaware, mumbling nonsense the whole time. Poor Petros comes to see me whenever his grandpa lets him, but obviously the sight is too frightening for him to approach or speak to me: he just fixes me with those big brown eyes of his, hoping in vain that the corpse he's seeing will assume his mother's form again. My heart goes out to him, but I can't even manage to sit up and hold him. Plus, I reek of anise: the whole room is suffused with fumes from the ouzo that's burning a hole in my insides.

Only once does he ask, eyeing the empty bottles gleaming in the dimness: "Mum? What are you drinking?" and I somehow succeed to surface from my delirious state and reply: "Almond cordial."

My dealings with Tassos are lengthier, exhausting; kneeling by my side, he strokes my head and begs me to pull myself together for our boy's sake. He assures me that I'm not a murderess as I keep saying in my half-sleep, that no one would ever dream of blaming me for what happened and that he's forgiven me and can't wait for the three of us to go back home and be a happy family like before. *Happy family. Before.* Yeah, right.

At least my father's visits, though painful, last only a few seconds. Every morning, after Tassos and the boy are gone, he comes into my room, closes the door behind him, and after standing silent above me for a few moments, starts kicking me – softly but insistently, like you'd kick a piece of trash stuck to the sole of your shoe.

"Get up, bitch," he says. "Get up and look after the child."

The Joy and the Indomitable Pain

Ah, they were the best of times, these wretched days!

The summers are bearable. Then, at least, the kid can go in the sea as much as he likes, and recently he's discovered yet another pastime he can share with his father: snorkelling. I'm sick with worry, of course, that the spear gun Tassos takes with him might misfire and pierce my angel's body and then I'll kill him with my bare hands, but the boys both seem to have such a tremendous time that I shut my mouth and cook the mussel rice they're so fond of; though by now I've grown so sick of mussels and octopus I can barely look at them.

Petros in his swimsuit is sadly what you'd call plump and I mind terribly about it; he's even grown breasts. But every time I'm about to tell him to go easy on the sweets, I remember the appetite stimulants I used to give him and once more I say nothing. Serves you right, stupid woman.

And there's also this kid in the village where we spend the summer of 1987, whose look I don't like one bit, what with the long hair and the cheap necklaces and bracelets he wears. The two of them disappear into fields and forests and basements together; God knows what sort of games they're playing. The thought that they might touch or fondle each other makes me want to jump off the balcony (since I'm such a huge failure: I've managed to make my son a fat, gay mummy's boy) or grab the other kid's mother and tear half her hair out for letting her boy, two years older than Petros, seduce my son. (As you may well imagine, gone are the books by Freud and Melanie Klein and the theories about the latency stage. I'm not yet aware that this word exists, but I deserve another epithet aside from *crazy*; I'm also one hell of a homophobe.)

It's the summer of 1988 – I don't even remember the exact date, ungrateful cow that I am – and suddenly Dad is gone, although he'd been gone for quite a while really. His dementia had advanced to a state where, despite the full-time nurse we'd hired to look after him, he was out of control – cursing or hitting her, leaving the house and wandering the streets lost and disoriented, the whole nine yards. So what did we do about it, we four kids whom he had taken care of as best he could (shops for Myron and Agis, homes for me and Cleo)? We found the cheapest old folks' home we could, a place as shabby and dreary as a makeshift grave, and we left him there to rot, literally, from the sepsis he suffered as a result of long-untended bedsores. The one time Petros went to see his grandpa there, he cried all the way back, saying over and over: "Why can't we take him to live with us, Mum? He can sleep in my bed, there's plenty of room!" But my siblings and I are complete and utter monsters. On the day of his death, after shedding half a tear each at most, we send our husbands and wives to clean up the mess – we don't even want to see him. And then something amusing happens. Since Agis lives closest to the cemetery, his in-laws offer to take care of clothing to dress the dead man, and Agis's mother-and-law accidentally takes a pair of shoes that Agis doesn't wear anymore, along with a shabby suit of her husband's. When Agis finds out he goes bananas, because aside from obsessive-compulsive he's also extremely superstitious and the thought that a corpse (even his father's) will be wearing *his* shoes while he's rotting in the ground means for him a potentially fatal case of bad luck. So poor Tassos is sent in a hurry to find shoes for his dead father-in-law and take them to the cheapest funeral parlour in the Balkans. Such a wonderful bunch, the Horianos kids.

And after the dead man's buried in haste and practically unmourned, my siblings will commit the coarsest act of treason yet against their youngest sister: for even though neither of our parents has left a will, everyone knows that our old place belongs to the 'runt of the litter' (that's what our mother said continually, and Tassos wanted me to take her to a notary but I called him a shameless gold-digger). The boys have the shop and dozens of acres of farmland, Cleo three apartments and the two stores Dad had opened for her useless first two husbands, whereas all I've got is our small apartment. And yet the three of them forget about all this in a split second. Our childhood home is sold for a song, and we split the paltry proceeds four ways. During the following days, I'll spend nearly half of it on gifts for Petros, my nieces and my nephews. This makes me feel like a better person than them, a generous, magnanimous soul, and so I forgive them. *Idiot. Fucking idiot.*

It's incredible, though, how money goes to your head. During the one and a half years that my tiny fortune lasts (Tassos will struggle to convince me to put some of the money away to buy a small seaside lot), I feel stronger than ever, invincible almost: gone are the phobias and the depression and the brooding about dead babies. Now I'm constantly buying things for Petros, and on the days when I'm too lazy to cook, I just take him to some posh restaurant in the evening, as if he is my diminutive lover. That's what a proper housewife does: her child is feasting on Peking duck while her husband starves to death, coming home to an empty fridge and a whole lot of nothing on the stove.

And Petros reciprocates my supposedly adult adoration tenfold, passing the entrance examination for the Anatolia College high school with flying colours without a single hour of studying, and acquiring within a couple of years both the Cambridge Certificate of Proficiency and the Sorbonne *diplôme*. He even entertains thoughts of studying in Paris and I encourage him, knowing fully well that if and when the dreaded time comes and he decides to study abroad, I'll have a breakdown to prevent him from going.

The only thing troubling me is a sour-faced maths teacher at school who gives Petros a hard time because he's '*too distracted*' in class, and it's all I can do during the PTA meeting not to find the bitch and give her a black eye for calling my son names.

And another thing: as if his being chubby weren't bad enough – I mean, I'm always pressuring him with some new diet, but then it breaks my heart to see the poor lamb gazing hungrily at TV commercials for ice cream – it seems my boy will also end up on the short side. He's already the second-shortest boy in his class (a mere four foot eleven at the age of thirteen!) and although I'm itching to give him some growth hormone, his father won't hear of it. "Nonsense!" he says. "I didn't reach my full height until I was twenty-two. You're not going to turn our child into your lab rat."

He's also turned out to be short-sighted, saying he can't see the numbers on the blackboard and that's why he's bad at maths, so he has to wear glasses. Bullshit. I'm sure his eyesight is flawless – both Tassos and I have 20/20 vision – and it's just a matter of insecurity. He feels short and fat and unpopular (being in the school choir doesn't help, especially as a boy soprano), he's biting his nails to the quick and now wishes to hide behind a pair of spectacles. I know because I, too, bought a pair of fake glasses when I was in high school, which I wore as a sort of shield – better to be called *four-eyes* than *loony*.

But I give him a break after all he's been through because of me.

During these eventful years, when I could feel content with the joys that Petros gives me, while trying to mend my waning relationship with Tassos, I commit the ultimate irresponsibility in regard to my disorder – something I know for a fact that many other manic-depressives also do, although this doesn't alleviate my own guilt one bit. When I feel fine, that is when I can manage on two hours of sleep and cook three meals a day and read and listen to music and even go to the gym and flirt with Vlassis the yoga instructor, then I go off my pills. I don't even take the lithium tablets which Dr Lemonis has sworn me to be mindful of. "Oh, go screw yourself, you pill-dispensing quack," is my civilized reply. And so, a couple of months at most after wearing myself out, the depression inevitably hits me like a stack of bricks and once more I'm sleeping on the floor and popping pills by the handful, washed down with beer which, shameless junkie that I am, I send Petros to fetch me from the kiosk.

It's only natural then that this mishandling of my illness leads to outbursts and situations that bring my poor boys to their wits' end.

For instance:

In the winter of 1990, I convince myself beyond the shadow of a doubt (and without a shred of proof, of course) that Tassos doesn't spend the evenings at the Aero Club as he claims when he's late home, but is screwing a trashy young cardiologist who recently started working at the hospital. And though he's denied my accusations and sworn that he wouldn't go anywhere near this woman even if they paid him to, I remain steadfast in my conviction that he's two-timing me. So, what do I do? One fine morning, when the boy gets up to go to school and sees me in the hallway and says: "Morning, Mum," I reply with a cool demeanour, as if I don't know him: "I'm not Mum. I'm the cardiologist." Terrified, Petros runs to his father and tells him; Tassos finds me in the bathroom, peeing. "Katerina? What's the boy talking about?" "I'm not Katerina," I say. "I'm the cardiologist." It may sound funny, but I keep this going for three days straight, despite my son's tears and his attempts to hug me – I just look away, push him off, and say: "I'm not your mother.

I'm the cardiologist." So on the fourth day, in order to protect his son's sanity, Tassos empties a vial of Haldol in my coffee, and after a day of zombification I come to my senses. The three months that I'm on antipsychotics, despite the Akineton I'm also taking to combat the parkinsonian side effects they have, I literally turn into an undead husk, staring emptily while my mouth is chewing on stale air, and grow emaciated since I'm unable to feed or dress myself without the help of my husband and son.

And then to cap it all, in the winter of 1991, Zoë suddenly dies. Feeling like I lost my true mother and my only backup for taking care of Petros now that I'm so incapable, I first make a half-hearted suicide attempt (it's Petros who finds me this time, and he manages to call for an ambulance despite his panic – luckily I get off with having my stomach pumped and receiving the worst earful ever from Tassos), and then go on a secret hunger strike, drinking only water, pitchers and pitchers of it, hoping to moisten my mouth which is always dry and sticky from the psych meds – until I suffer a thing I didn't even know existed called *water poisoning*. That means my electrolytes are so severely screwed-up after five days of starvation and over-hydration that one night I wake up, vomit a river of watery bile, and then lose consciousness. Fortunately, Tassos is coolheaded enough to give me mouth-to-mouth resuscitation and CPR, while the boy, awakened by his father's justified curses, stands at the bedroom door with a pillow pressed against his face so the neighbours won't hear his uncontrollable sobbing at three in the morning.

And then the craziest stunt of them all, which we were lucky to survive.

It's the spring of 1992 and Tassos flies off, with my blessing, for a two-day trip to Istanbul along with some of his Aero Club buddies. And as, that same night, he doesn't pick up when I call his hotel room, I'm convinced he's not there with friends but with a girlfriend. (Despite the proof I'm going to get from the photos that belie my jealous scenarios and show Tassos grinning at a club with his co-pilot and two male passengers, not suspecting the ordeal in store for him…) I act as the loving and devoted wife on the phone and Tassos returns from the airport on Monday morning to have a shower, change and leave for the hospital. He asks me to iron a shirt for him and, while Petros is in his room playing some computer game or other, I take a shirt from the bedroom closet, hang it up on the wooden coat rack in the hall, douse it with pure alcohol and set fire to it. By the time the boys realise what's happening from the stink and the smoke, the coat rack is burning furiously, while tongues of fire are licking at the hall ceiling and melting the plastic folding living-room door. As for me, I just sit there, with a look on my face like a deranged Nero, gazing triumphantly at the flames.

This arsonist stunt costs me a week at the clinic. Serves me right.

And during all these years, each and every day, no matter how happy I am, I'll still hear them: the tiny, bare feet of my unborn daughter running across the hall; the racket from the nursery; the kiddie programs on TV, the songs learnt at school, the lisping, gap-toothed words; the high-pitched voice, the gleeful laugh.

That first "Mummy!" I'll never hear again.

The Love Lives of My Husbands

After all those years of substance abuse and daily psychic squalor, the last remaining embers of my youthful libido go out:

by now I am frigid and I know I'm frigid because I don't mind it one bit. I feel as if I've escaped once and for all from a chore – thus denouncing my onetime joy like all bitter and miserable people tend to do – which was never worth the trouble to begin with. Going to the gym, dieting, dressing up and painting my face – and all this, for what? To awaken Tassos's desire which has been slumbering for years, at least when it comes to me? Nowadays, all he sees when he looks at me even on my good days is a version of his mother, as unthinkable as a sexual partner as Chryssoula with her stuffed-bird stare.

Of course, I've long accepted the fact that a man like Tassos, even more handsome now that he's turned forty, will seek elsewhere the love he doesn't find at home: it's natural, reasonable, just and humane, and it shatters my heart into pieces. But why?

Because I'm afraid that someday I'll go too far and lose him. I know that our marriage and his presence at my side are in his mind ineradicable features of his time-honoured role as husband and father, but still… The kid's growing up; by now, when Tassos and I quarrel, he mostly reacts with indifference and sometimes, in order to punish me after some stunt or other, he spends a couple of nights at his office. Petros, seeing both of us much calmer when separated and twice as prone to dote on him out of guilt, prefers it to the everyday bickering he's grown sick of enduring ever since he was little. And yet if Tassos leaves for good, it'll kill me; already these two-day absences result in nights of drinking myself into a stupor while Petros is away spending the night with his father.

And so I imagine several mistresses – it matters little whether they really exist or not – and hate them for their allure, their independence, their guts and the sexual passion they can experience and provoke. I eavesdrop on Tassos's phone calls while I'm lying in bed, pretending to be conked out from the pills, and I could swear he's talking to his girlfriend – that hazy girlfriend of my masochistic imaginings, that woman of a hundred faces and the thousand charms I lack.

We're not a couple anymore. Just roommates – if that.

For a long time, my husband has been Petros.

It is to him I bare my soul, complain and tell stories, things about my tempestuous past no thirteen-year-old boy should know about his mother. Besides making him my beer mule, I've also turned him into my psych meds co-conspirator: in order to be always well-stocked in pills, I send him secretly every now and then to buy me those that don't require a prescription. I give him books on seduction to read: books by Marguerite Duras, Anaïs Nin, Karen Blixen and Germaine Greer – loose women, lascivious and bisexual women who speak about love with titillating precision. Needless to say, he is allowed to smoke and drink whatever he finds lying about in the house.

However, I know that my belated efforts to turn him into a lover of women are doomed to failure. For the past two years he's been best friends with a boy at school who is infamous for his rowdy behaviour and the fact of not only being openly gay, but acting in as effeminate a manner as possible in order to provoke the fury of those who taunt him. The two of them have become inseparable, and they've discovered common obsessions, like their love for old Hollywood movies: every other day they're camped out in the living room, watching film noir and Oscar-winning blockbusters, while wolfing down anything they can lay their hands on: they're both quite chubby and they'd be perfectly adorable were I not convinced that each one is corrupting the other.

For instance, slow in every facet of his growth aside from his mental acuity, Petros recently discovered the joys of self-pleasure and he's going at it like crazy: whereas it was always a trial to get him to bathe, now he spends hours in the shower with the bathroom door locked. And I don't mind that he's jerking off: he's a teenage boy, what is he supposed to do with his dick, pickle it? What drives a knife through my heart is a) who taught him how to do it, if he didn't chance upon it on his own, and b) whether they're doing it together. Quite simply, I worry about what he might be up to with his bosom buddy behind closed doors.

I've already sniffed out the magazines he's meticulously concealed at the back of his bottom drawer and it was all I could do not to rip them to shreds or jump off the balcony, haunted by the revolting things they portray. In the end I just burst into tears, my hands filled with gay porn: the pathetic failure, the despicable mother who didn't get one thing right.

And yet I find it impossible to broach the subject with him and equally impossible to accept it. How will I manage not to kill myself if, ashamed and angry, he turns and tells me to my face that it's my fault, that the reason he's gay is the unhealthy relationship I've cultivated between us ever since he was a baby?

If all this is not just a phase of experimentation – as I pray every single night – I only hope that he'll manage to tame his urges, or turn them into something beautiful and tender, like the songs of Hadjidakis. And he's shown signs of being on the right track: he's already reading and writing poetry in three languages, and has set many of his poems to music, playing them on the piano that succeeded the old Yamaha keyboard.

How I love his singing voice, and the melancholy songs he composes! How filled with pride I am, and how ashamed I feel for not loving him unconditionally, without being appalled by a side of his psyche that might have been simply made thus, by something as natural perhaps as his lovely brown eyes! Why am

I seeking perfection on my terms when what stands before me is perfect in every way? Why am I so ungrateful?

No, I'm not fooling myself with excuses about my own youth, when the vast majority of homosexuals were doomed to a lifetime of scorn, alienation and loneliness. Things are changing each and every day; it's everywhere: in the music and film industries, in literature, even in sports and politics. If people as admirable and eminent as Clive Barker, k.d. lang and Martina Navratilova can be openly gay and still be accepted, there's no reason why my son should end up lonely and miserable.

But no matter how lucidly I reason about it while trying to convince myself, the perversity of maternal despotism is all-powerful: when the three of us go to watch Ang Lee's *The Wedding Banquet*, I rush out of the cinema in the middle of the film, jump into a taxi, go home and get plastered, and when Tassos and Petros ask worriedly what happened, I start yelling at them to leave me alone, that I just had a panic attack.

Like his father, where the nonexistence of our sex life is never discussed and I'm still pretending (not always successfully) that I don't care if he sticks his dick into the socket, the other man who lives with me under a regime of erotic incompatibility will also be doomed to ten years of guilt-ridden silence and by his own mother no less, who'd been his companion and confidante for years, and whose consoler and unofficial therapist he still is. A silence that will breed self-blame and so many other monsters: the monster of pathological obesity, the monster of rebellious sexual hyperactivity, sign of a man who is in denial and constant repression, and also the monster of a grotesque, unnatural wedding (my idea) with a lovely girl whom I will also condemn to a lifetime of sexual loneliness. And all this because I longed to cure my son and have, if not grandchildren, at least the daughter I had killed. This girl had such a big heart that she would love me nevertheless and travel all the way across Europe to attend my funeral, grieving as if she had lost her own mother.

Maybe, deep down, I wasn't so bad after all.

The Horrors of Others: Rachel

Despite my father's objections and preposterous accusations, Mrs Campanile was, right to the end, my mother's best and closest friend: a kind, gentle and generous soul, married to Saul, an equally kindly and loveable man. Having no children of her own, Rachel always doted on the Horianos clan like a loving aunt and years later she became more of a grandmother to Petros than Mama Rini herself.

I can almost see her, stepping out of the dark mists of nothingness: white hair, a wrinkled, smiling face, and a perfumed handkerchief tucked into the left sleeve of her blouse, to conceal the faded but still visible death camp tattoo.

That she and her husband were survivors of Auschwitz was something my siblings and I knew ever since we were little and we were strictly forbidden to mention this dark past in front of Rachel.

However, being kids, we were naturally curious to find out more about this fascinating chapter of history: Auntie Rachel and Uncle Saul imprisoned in a concentration camp? How could one reconcile the image of these two frail, kind, soft-spoken elderly people with the most chilling and methodically brutal kind of horror ever devised by the human race?

And how did they ever manage to survive when millions perished?

The explanation we'd been given, during a hush-hush visit upstairs which we never told Mum about, was that the couple had escaped the ovens because of their musical gift; even now, Saul was a wonderful piano player, and Rachel's voice, though ravaged by age, bore witness to the nightingale splendour of her youthful singing. So, instead of killing them, their Auschwitz wardens had used them as entertainers, which kept them alive till the end of the war and the liberation of the camps.

However, as an adolescent, during one of my frequent visits to the library I had stumbled upon a book called *House of Dolls*, written by an anonymous Jewish author and death camp survivor, which revealed in shocking detail the 'joy divisions' – what a horrid euphemism – where hundreds of attractive young women were forced into the life of a sex slave, working night and day in makeshift brothels. And combining this terrible knowledge together with Rachel's old photos which showed a woman of resplendent beauty, I realized what an inconceivable ordeal this admirable, warm and forgiving old lady had been through.

And I remember Petros as a child listening to Rachel's own account of survival – changing the version slightly, making herself a gifted seamstress – and wondering at her strength, her perseverance and dignity.

Yet nothing could prepare me for the staggering truth.

It is the winter of 1994 and Rachel, almost a hundred years old but still quite lucid, a childless widow with only a few relatives scattered in Switzerland and France, has fallen into the claws of Cleo, who has ingratiated herself with the old woman in hopes of being included in her will. My shameless sister even calls her *Mummy Rachel,* something that makes me laugh out loud and at the same time feel nauseous at the thought that this vile person is my own sister.

After a lot of brown-nosing, she manages to inherit a poky apartment in a warehouse district of the city, where, among crates of old junk, she unearths a small satchel containing a heap of old notebooks. And since they're all written in French and Cleo wouldn't go anywhere near any form of reading even in her worst nightmare, she asks me whether I'd care to keep them. Out of curiosity I do.

It is thus that I find myself reading a chronicle of Rachel's four-year imprisonment and torture, including descriptions that makes my blood run cold. The reason she never had children, I learn, wasn't a matter of choice, but the result of a sterilization process enforced upon the Jewish women the Germans used as prostitutes, which consisted of numerous electroshock discharges applied directly to the cervix.

When Petros finds me shaking and sobbing and drinking gin straight from the bottle, he asks me what's wrong and I recount Rachel's horrific story. And while I'm telling my son all about it, I realize the reason this tale of torment has devastated me so: I'm still carrying around the secret of our true origins.

Petros initially reacts with disbelief — how reliable is a mother who, drunk out of her mind, mumbles about Jewish great-grandmothers? — and then with denial; he doesn't want to carry any more baggage, especially if it all comes down to something as negligible as one-eighth of his genetic makeup.

I'll throw the notebooks away — I can't bear having them in the house — but their elaborate handwriting has been etched indelibly onto my soul, making me hate myself even more. Here was a woman who, though sterilized by her tormentors, managed to be sweet and loving and forbearing, whereas I, monstrous I, went and sterilized myself for reasons which, compared to Rachel's past, seem petty and stupid and base.

When this woman went through so much and managed to survive, what gives me the audacity to think every other day about committing suicide?

I wish we could be saved by the miseries of others – but like their happiness, when you're struggling with your own despair and solitude, their pain seems indifferent, alien.

Do you know what it feels like to loathe yourself so much, that –

I know, Katerina. Shut up.

Days of Croissants and Prayers

Dear God, please help my son get accepted in the Medical School here in Thessaloniki.

Dear God, help him get well. And if Your Will is that he stays that way, make him be happy, and let him stay close to me forever.

Dear God, please protect my poor weary mind. Don't let me go mad.

Dear God, please forgive my crimes. Don't condemn me to Hell.

These are my nightly prayers, which I utter silently while kneeling on the bedroom's old hardwood floor, until my knees start to bleed and grow scabby – so across the floor I have to lay cardboard boxes which used to contain pre-packaged croissants – twelve per box. Poor Tassos carts them off from the discount supermarket every day and rarely gets a taste of them. You see, Petros is studying for his university entrance exam, and the two of us are eating like a pair of pregnant manatees. We've grown to bestial proportions: I weigh one hundred and eighty pounds and Petros more than two hundred by now. But it's a small, puny price compared to the reward and the unimaginable joy of having him study here in Thessaloniki, until he finds the cure for cancer and gets his Nobel and declares in his acceptance speech, "*Mamma, this is for you!*" For this is what he's been calling me, *Mamma,* ever since we saw Fellini's *Amarcord,* and he learned how to play Nino Rota's heavenly score on the piano for me.

During the last couple of years I've calmed down considerably, almost to the point of a healthy equanimity. Just as, when Petros was sixteen, everything seemed about to fall apart – my relationship with Tassos and its effects on the boy: every now and then he'd drink himself stupid and his place at his high school was in constant peril because of his conduct, so that the teachers who were fond of and sorry for him had to defend him to the principal almost on a daily basis for cursing and smoking and doing God knows what in the men's room – this blessed exam came along and we've all found our purpose in life: his father is prematurely and insanely proud of him (for deep down he knows what kind of genius I've raised), Petros is studying as much as he can (he barely gets four hours of sleep, the poor lamb; he wakes up while it's still dark to solve physics and chemistry problems), and I've finally found a round-the-clock occupation: overseeing Petros's studying, listening to him recite entire textbooks he's memorized from cover to cover, and so, now that I have a goal that keeps me busy once more, I don't need beer or pills or anything else, only food and sweets, especially the syrup-soaked Turkish sweets my darling Eel brings us, after driving all the way into the city to buy them.

Oh, yes, I forgot to tell you about the pet name I've recently coined for Tassos, something I last did in the mid-Seventies, when we were still in love. But in this belated serenity that reigns over my soul, I've found out that I can love him again, if not as passionately as back then, at least with all the gratitude I owe him for everything he's done and endured. So, because he's constantly finding or making up reasons to slither away from me and out my grasp (anything to be away from home, and who could blame him, poor guy?) I call him teasingly The Eel, but I say it sweetly, as an endearment, so he too finds it funny. Sometimes when we're talking on the phone I'm overcome with uxorious emotion and call him Eelie, and he calls me Baby Chubs because I've become massive and also because I'm constantly wearing this old-fashioned white nightgown that Petros brought me from London and after spending hours glued to my leather armchair, the back of the gown sticks to my gigantic bum whenever I deign to get up. So now I'm Baby Chubs. (And with hindsight I realize how right he was when he used to say that my siblings and I ended up broken like this because of our idleness, of the fact that, having nothing to do, we just kept rehashing the minutiae of our neurotic misery. And here I am, being healthy thanks to having something to do: namely, to make sure my son becomes the greatest doctor in history).

And there's so much love bursting inside me, there's even enough for things I was certain I could never come to love – like Petros's homosexuality. Sure, I might pray that it's all just a phase, but the more I think about it, the more I come to see there's really nothing wrong with it. On the contrary, he'll always stay close to me. Look at Tassos's brother: he's been living for twenty years with his adorable, kind-hearted Moroccan partner, but he still takes his laundry to his mum and every Sunday he and the boyfriend have dinner at his parents'. Would I prefer it if some cheap hussy seduced my Petros and caused him to tank his exams? Not in a million years – he's better off being gay, never mind the fact that everyone knows gay men are smarter and more gifted and have tons of girlfriends, more than any macho man. And even if he does end up all alone, he'll always have me. This is an egotistical, petty thought and I often add it to the sins for which I ask forgiveness in my nightly prayers, but on the other hand it seems reasonable that Petros won't be able to find himself a man. And not because he's a bit roly-poly; he simply *doesn't know* how to love a man. He doesn't even know how to love his own father: the two of them have been getting on each other's nerves since Petros was a little boy, or else are too indifferent towards one another to bother finding ways to bond. But even if he never finds a man who'll love him – and what do men know about love, anyway? All they ever think about is what goes on below the waist – I'll always be here, a rock, my heart forever whispering *Petros, Petros, Petros*. Or, as I started to call him recently "my blue opossum with the pink feathers". It's somewhat babyish and… gay, I admit it, and the Eel doesn't approve at all ("What kind of baby talk is that to a grown man?") but Petros seems to like it – and who doesn't enjoy a flashback to one's infancy? I, for one, love it.

And thus, reminiscing about the good old days and trying to forget the misery they held, during this blessed lull I've even managed to love my hateful, disgusting self – or at least to get used to it, since I'm going to live with it as long as my son is there with me. And I, who was always counting my faults and errors and everything that rendered me deficient in the eyes of others but even more so in mine, now suddenly find that I'm not so horrible after all. Besides, if Petros loves me, if his face lights up whenever he says "*Mamma!*", then I must have done something good in my life. I may have been sick and difficult and bitter and selfish, but still I managed to do something many women (my sister, for example) fail miserably at: I raised a child with so much love and confidence in himself that it seems there's nothing he can't do; he speaks, reads and writes fluently in two languages, improvises wonderful melodies on the piano without ever having taken a single music lesson, and in ten or twenty years the whole world will talk about his medical achievements. It's not a small thing being the proud mother of a brilliant kid. Proud and happy. That's what I keep reminding myself the hours Petros and I spend together studying or watching all those depressing European movies he loves so much (Imagine! There was a time when I was the one educating him in the fine arts), the Fassbinder and Bergman films whose depiction of dysfunction makes our own fucked-up family pale in comparison. And who knows? Maybe one day he'll even give me a grandkid – I don't know how, but nowadays anything's possible, and all the women will lust after him, even if he doesn't care for them – a happy Katerinaki who'll always be laughing. Always.)

So at night I drop to my sore, enormous knees upon the flattened cardboard boxes we have emptied of their fattening goods, and pray to a God in whom I believe only when I need him and who will certainly grant my wishes because he was the father of an only son as well and preached love above all. And then, at three in the morning when everybody's asleep, I tiptoe to the doorway of the room where my other God sleeps, the God I love with even greater fervour, and who is equally omnipotent in the way he rules my heart, my mind, my soul. *Mamma*, he says, and I am born again. *Mamma*, and I forget the meaning of the word misery.

My prayers will be answered and Petros will pass his exam and be accepted at the Medical School of Thessaloniki. Before I know it he'll be a doctor, and I'll be full of pride, swollen with elation.

Though before any of that comes to pass, my strange, brilliant child will once more stray from the life I've been imagining for him. He's never to become a doctor after all, even if I'm not aware of it at the time – he's barely aware of it himself, as he chisels away at his first short stories, which he'll keep hidden from everyone for nearly two years. Not a saviour of lives, then, but an inventor of lives: a storyteller.

Corpses, Clinics, Weed and Lust

A newcomer to Medical School – and even more of an inexperienced newcomer to love – Petros will meet Patroclus from Crete, a blond-maned Adonis a year older than him, and from the first day they meet they'll be bound with invisible ropes of attraction.

Patroclus is clearly more worldly than my son, and, like many provincial youths, he doesn't feel the slightest shame about who he is and what he desires – plus he's so handsome and manly, you can't keep your eyes off of him. He smokes filterless cigarettes, drinks strong black coffee and has a permanently insolent expression. It's only when he sees my baby that he softens up, opening up as a flower to the sun.

It's not enough that they're together at classes all the time, or that each and every night Petros stays until two at Patroclus's place – staggering back home in the dead of night, woozy with heartache – but they also spend every single moment they're apart on the phone, whispering and laughing and humming songs to one another, so much so that Tassos in on his case nonstop.

"I don't like this guy one bit," he says.

"Oh, he's not bad, I can tell. And they're just friends. You always tend to think the worst."

"Just remember the photos I showed you."

As if I could forget them, unsee them, goddamn that Internet that keeps them glued to the computer all day long. For Tassos discovered some photos Petros had forgotten to delete from his Internet history (whatever the hell that means), depicting men doing the beast with two backs and he just had to print them up and show them to me, so that I can't get rid of their afterimage no matter how hard I try. That's what he's doing with Patroclus? (Of course, Katerina. Did you think they were just playing backgammon, two healthy young men in their bloom?)

For me it's more than enough that my boy is happy and smiling again; even if he reeks of pot every now and then, for I've smoked the occasional joint in my own youth and recognize the smell. Big deal, we're Greeks, people are getting stoned left and right. On the other hand, being both gay and a pothead is perhaps too much. At least the Cretan comes from a good right-wing family, so we're spared the 'communist' bit, as Zoe would say, God bless her soul. And, above all, a doctor.

They're both studying pretty hard, they're smart, and they've even picked out their future vocations: Petros will become a coroner and Patroclus a shrink. His clothes are suffused with the stench of the morgue where both of them hang out every morning, the excuse being they're free to smoke in there. Lucky thing that Petros is so in love and showering all the time, otherwise he'd be stinking to high heaven.

It would be nice if Petros became a shrink as well – he'd be able to prescribe my pills, and who knows, maybe one day he'd manage to convince me to go into therapy. But so long as he's happy and safe and loved, I don't give a hoot what sort of callisthenics he's doing with Patroclos behind closed doors.

Just before the second year of their studies begins, the rotten brats pull off a stunt that scares us to death: they book tickets to London and disappear for five whole days, during which we're beside ourselves with worry, not knowing whom to call and what to report, for Petros was too crafty to be talked into a cell phone – he didn't want us to be able to track his movements. After a couple of days we call Patroclus' parents, who are equally frantic, and on day five we start calling hospitals and police stations when, all of a sudden, the phone rings and Petros, speaking in English for emphasis, announces that he's in London, he's not coming back, and he'll live there with Patroclus for the rest of his days. Medicine bores him to death, he declares, he'll study English Literature, preferably in Oxford.

I'm numb with terror at this prospect, barely able to hold the receiver to my ear, when Tassos, bless him, retorts: "Well, I hope that aside from your talent for writing, you also have a hidden talent for dishwashing," he says (the shameless opossum has never washed a single dish in his whole life), "because that's what you'll be doing up there – you're not seeing another penny from us."

And so, tails between their legs, the amorous couple returns, and after a couple of months they split up, for the Cretan has rekindled some old flame back in his hometown, and my poor baby is crying his eyes out, listening to *No Need to Argue* round the clock, which is too depressing for comfort for all its charms. And Tassos blames me for listening with our son to all those corny songs he loves so much now!

There's going to be a lot of bitter fighting far worse than this in the years to come, especially between father and son – for Petros soon enough abandons the dream of becoming any kind of doctor, since he's secretly sent his stories to a publisher and they're actually coming out this June, though under a pen name.

Now my son has two names, like a Mafioso. I am indescribably proud and even Tassos, though he won't admit it, keeps harassing anyone who crosses the threshold of his practice with newspaper clippings of reviews so they can see what kind of son he has, while Petros, during his sleepless nights, keeps pouring out his wounded soul into yet more stories and books. Or, rather, I should say *Auguste* does.

But sometimes books hide wounds – literally. Because, while he uses the computer regularly, he writes his own poems, or the ones which he translates, longhand with the pen his father and I gave him when he was accepted at Medical School.

And one day, while browsing at his bookshelves for something French to read, in order to dust off my French somewhat, I see a piece of paper sticking out of the pages of a brown hardcover volume. I take it down and see it's a collection of poems by Philip Larkin. My English is a bit rusty, but the page in question is a translation into Greek Petros has done of a poem called *This Be the Verse*. It's in his handwriting, written, oddly enough, with a red pen.

Perhaps I ought to have considered it private, and not read it.

No, not perhaps – for sure. I thought, you see, that my boy was happy, now that he'd found something to do – a job that satisfies his soul and opens doors (which will take him away from me, even though I will be further away still).

Those lines stab me where it hurts the most. They begin:

They fuck you up, your mum and dad
They may not mean to, but they do.

Ah, Philip, the things you knew!
And the things I have yet to learn.

Like a Crumbling Tower

The first time that depression will overwhelm Petros will be a few days before the attack on the Twin Towers on September 11th, 2001.

That horrendous maternal heritage will manage, within a month's time, to rob him of his smile, to make him shed twenty pounds because he feels his throat closing up and cannot swallow a bite, and to spend most of his days and nights lying in bed, staring at the ceiling, unbathed to the point that Tassos and I are wondering whether we should take him out on the balcony and wash him with the garden hose.

And how does the lunatic mother feel seeing her son suffering from a disease she passed on to him with the very milk she breast-fed him?

On the one hand, I am devastated.

Yet on the other, I feel once more omnipotent, just like I did when he depended on me for everything. So now, despite his twenty-two years, he's regressed to infanthood, dozing all day long and occasionally letting out a soft, croaky "*Mamma!*" so I feed him some water or puréed fruit, the only things that can pass through his constricted pharynx, whose pathology neither the internist nor the ENT specialist have managed to determine, and which I know for certain is just a physical manifestation of depression.

His only pleasure is playing the piano, where, stooped and silent, he tinkles away at the heartrending songs of his teenage years. There's one song in particular called 'Annabel Lee', set to Poe's last poem from what he's told me, and whenever he plays it I have to pretend I'm overtaken by a sudden urge to pee, so I can dart out of the living room, lest the poor baby see the tears in my eyes and becomes even sadder.

Oh, and he smokes too much, my God, he's always puffing away, so his once angelic voice has grown as hoarse as Mum's when she had to speak through the oxygen mask.

And I, just as greedily, along with his cigarette smoke and his musical anguish, inhale his helplessness, and the joy it brings me, shame on me, I guess, but I don't give a shit anymore. Do you know how it feels to have your kid need you so, to cling to you, to be his only company and solace at night when he barely manages to swallow the spoonful of custard I feed him, so he won't grow sick from malnourishment? Love means bearing crosses.

And if they're not there, being able to invent them.

This Book

This book does not intend to hurt anyone but those who read it.

This book, they'll say, is filled with lies, with malicious inaccuracies, it is an attempt to sully the reputation of an entire family by a mind both unstable and rancorous, seeking to avenge the death it brought upon itself.

Yet this is my own truth. Everyone is free to choose the oblivion they desire, the one that comforts them – it is so, if they think so.

This book is tearing me apart. This book's purpose is to tear me apart, to cut me into pieces.

In my pieces I am whole.

The Horrors of Others: Whatever Happened to the Horianos Siblings?

Of my three siblings, I only ever truly loved Agis. However, every time Myron or Cleo needed me I was there for them, not as a sister but like a mother – right to the very end, regardless of the cost. My home was always open to them, even though it was the smallest: it was in my living room that we had our gatherings, and on my sofa that every now and then all three of them would lie down and unburden their hearts, not caring whether I was strong enough to bear it: whenever they were crushed by depression, or tormented by their numerous neuroses, it was me they came weeping to. I was once more their Little Katerina and they loved me not only better than their other siblings, but even more than their own spouses. At times like these, I was kind and good and loveable. I was the best.

But woe to me when *I* was suffering from clinical depression, when I was on my hands and knees. Then they'd be gone in a flash, for days and months on end, as if I had typhus, cholera, the plague, and they might catch it. They didn't give a rat's arse how my husband and son were coping. Then, during the difficult times, I was Mad Katerina, and poor Tassos was a saint for not having me committed. They said all that behind my back, of course. They also envied my son because he made their own kids seem mediocre by comparison, and they never had a kind word or a loving gesture for him. *He'll turn out a nutcase as well. Tassos should have locked her up back in the 80s, when the poor kid still had a chance.*

That's why my suicide destroyed them. And still does.

Not that it was their fault – at least, no more than it was mine, when my own brain had turned against me.

Some bad gene, perhaps; a fatal mistake (or a hundred) in our upbringing. Or, as our tortured, forbearing spouses used to say, the fact that none of us had ever had to work for a living. Myron and Agis merely ran Dad's store to the ground, while Cleo and I just sat all day on our big fat arses doing nothing. At least my brothers and I spent time with our children, making sure they were getting the love we were deprived of, and that they'd achieve more in life than we had.

Yet look at us now, in our forties and fifties: four grownup men and women who are still each other's best friends. Middle-aged failures with no social life, who have always spent the holidays together, as if a heavy, rusty chain, instead of blood, bound us to one another: our illness and our unmentionable past.

No one will ever undergo proper psychotherapy: we're just a bunch of pill poppers who suffer regular, debilitating attacks.

Myron, near the end, following colossal losses in the stock market, will spend a month of daily sessions at my house, where he'll be lying on the sofa, with me seated behind him as an unofficial shrink, and regurgitate all his woes, reminding me of that awful fairy tale about a girl who confided nothing but moments of misery to her doll, until the doll became infested with maggots. I'd forgiven Myron's adolescent cruelty towards me long ago; since our mother always treated him like royalty, it was only natural to view us as his subjects in his reign of terror.

Agis, after a lifelong struggle with his own demons, will grow prematurely old. His wife Ritsa will be his rock and his guardian angel at tremendous personal and psychological cost, making sure their children want for nothing.

As for Cleo, words do not suffice. The periods when we're best friends and exchange daily visits to each other's home and stay up all night going on trips down memory lane will be punctuated by interludes of unprovoked and unforgivable viciousness on her part, especially when it comes to my marriage with Tassos. Countless times she's tried to split us up, badmouthing one to the other in moments of crisis, the same way she'll try and wreck the marriages of friends, relations and acquaintances (including those of her own kids; she won't even be invited to her son's wedding), until she ends up all alone and pitiable, an old lady with a pair of dentures made gratis by my husband, a woman who's been lying to herself and to others for so long, she has trouble remembering the truth anymore.

(Do you remember, sis, that time when Petros was in high school, and I had a fight with his father as usual, and you called me all choked up with the inconceivable lie that your daughter Irini, while lying back on her uncle's dental chair, felt him fondling her breast? You were stabbing your brother-in-law in the back, the same one to whom your son Minas confided his troubles, when his own father didn't give a shit for him. Do you recall that phone call? And poor Irini, who was listening on the extension, suddenly burst into tears and swore that nothing of the sort had ever happened. It was then that Tassos finally forbid you to ever set foot in our house again and it served you right; even though, a few months before I was gone, when you were so strapped for cash that you were starving, foolish me, I got Petros to drop me at your place with a car full of groceries. And you'll surely remember that other time, when during one of your quarrels, Agis told you: "The wrong sister died." Even though I disagree; it was right that I should die.)

Ladies and gentlemen, feel free to admire the wonders of a Greek family.

Sick, sick, sick.

I got out as early as I could.

Troublesome Twos

If I were a sun, I'd be setting. The year is 2002.

Two has always been a symbolic number in our family; but there'll be just two of us left this year.

One of them is my son, who will never die.

The other? My Tassos, my darling Eel, my Rock.

Do I know I'll be gone by the end of this year? Yes and no.

I want it badly, though. Even if the thought terrifies me sometimes.

However, what I fear most is the loss of myself, the waning of my mind which, after years of abuse, has begun to betray me.

I deserve to be canonized for everything I suffered this year.

Or burn in the deepest pit of Hell for all the harm I did to my child.

See, when you cease to exist, you stop worrying about a lot of things. Now I remember it as if everything happened to some strangers. Who *is* that Katerina?

I have yet to know.

January

And here comes the euro. Being slow in practical matters – all these years and I still don't know how to work the video, and now there's yet another contraption whose name I don't know. Til the day I die I will refer to euros as dollars with comical results, such as when I tell a taxi driver: "Oh, so sorry, I've got nothing smaller than a fifty-dollar bill," while he stares at me in the rearview mirror, thinking, *Enormous* and *stupid*.

I'm also becoming forgetful. Frequently. I might be

surrounded by ashtrays, have two cigarettes going at once, and light a third one – I'm smoking nearly five packs a day, and every morning when I wake up I cough up tar and feathers. The floor, the furniture, the curtains are filled with cigarette burns – I've even got some on my massive thighs. If anyone saw me naked, they'd think I've been tortured to renounce the Communist Party and then they'd faint from terror, because by now I've hit the big three hundred and when I undress to take a shower, I fear the bathroom mirror will crack of despair. Nowadays I dress solely in quadruple extra-large velvet sweat suits; I literally possess no other clothes – as Petros, distraught and astonished, will find out after my death, when the undertakers will be asking him for clothes to bury me in and he'll find only sweat suits spotted with cigarette burns in my wardrobe. I also forget that I'm farsighted now and, not wishing to admit that I'm getting old, I constantly pilfer Tassos's reading glasses, and when the poor Eel goes to his dental practice, he gives someone a crown instead of a filling.

Near the end of the month, Petros, refusing to study for his midterm exams, blurts out his plans about moving to Athens where most of his friends live; in any case he goes there every other month on account of his books. Even though I refrain from commenting, on that same night I gobble up five Seroxat tablets and get so tachycardic that I think my heart is about to explode. Tassos tells me to just take a couple of Valium with a beer and stop being hysterical, but I'm convinced the end is near, so I make Petros drive me to the hospital. However, as soon as we get there, I get scared. What if they think it's a suicide attempt and want to keep me for a three-day observation? So I just say I'm feeling better, which I really am, and could we just go grab some crepes because we shouldn't go to bed with an empty stomach, and so we end up driving around town, singing old Italian songs and wolfing down junk food.

My baby is never going away. Where will he ever have a grander time than right here with *Mamma?*

February

The Eel spending more and more evenings away from home (he's probably bonking some new girlfriend, but I couldn't care less), Petros and I spend a month of near-incestuous closeness. He tells me our relationship has long become symbiotic; I like the word. So I'm his – what? "Well, aside from the fact that we're not sleeping together, I'd pretty much go with *wife*," he replies. (God will strike us down any day now.)

After two in the morning, we pull on our coats over our pyjamas, put on our tattered trainers and drive to the casino, where we spend the rest of the night getting hammered and playing five-euro roulette and blackjack, because at six o' clock the breakfast buffet opens and we can pig out like there's no tomorrow. (*Is* there?)

We're even smoking the same brand of cigarettes: More Menthols, which Tassos objects to because they cost a fortune. Plus, "These are not masculine cigarettes," he says to Petros and he replies: "I've grown a beard. People will know."

This is my favourite two so far – just the two of us.

March

Following a short trip abroad, Petros goes on a crash diet, practically starving himself. Within a couple of months, he'll plummet from 320 pounds to 140. This metamorphosis fills us with joy and pride (my boy is finally handsome, and not in my own eyes alone), while at the same time terrifies me, for along with handsome comes sexy, and that means he could fall for some guy who lives in a faraway place and go after him and leave me here to rot. I can't relive the Cretan-kid nightmare all over again.

But it's my duty to help him in his efforts. For no matter how clingy I've become (practically a leech), deep down I know that he's grown up now and sooner or later he'll probably want – he *must* want – to move to his own place. I'm not planning on making him my life-long companion.

At least not consciously.

April

Because of some damned anti-inflammatory pill combined with his starvation regime, my poor boy suffers a bleeding of the stomach, as confirmed by a gastroscopy.

At first I panic – what if it's cancer? – but the surgeon who examines him is a friend of Tassos and reassures me it's something easily treatable.

And then begins the wonderful recovery period, during which I'm running back and forth bringing him milk and plumping up his pillows and making him grilled cheese sandwiches and overcooked spaghetti, and it's as if he's five again, depending on me for everything like last year when he got depressed, and his weakness fills me with strength and vitality.

So much wasted mothering. What a loss did I suffer when –

Oh no, no, no, Katerina, we're definitely *not* thinking about *that*. *That* is best left forgotten.

The worst moments are those when I really forget.

May

As if to express a gratitude too great to be uttered, Petros writes a novella, *Mona Lisa's Son*. Next day, at the end of the reading marathon – he reads it aloud to me, since I can no longer concentrate on books because of the pills – I am reduced to tears. Petros falls on his knees terrified and apologizes, saying he didn't want to upset me. It's the best gift a mother could ever receive from her son, I reassure him.

And I mean it, more or less.

Only this book tells the story of a middle-aged man who never knew his mother, who's never even seen a single photo of her. His mother is essentially a ghost who haunts him with her absence, her unknown face, until he is forced into an outrageous self-exile.

So I can't help wondering: Is that how my son sees me? Existing yet not existing? A stranger whose face he can't make out?

That's why I'm crying. Because the day will come when my son will have forgotten my face.

Because, as if I were already dead, he's seeking it in his writing with a sense of despair.

June

During a huge fight with his father, who calls him the cancer that eats away at our family – to which he answers back that he can't wait for Tassos to be dead so he can bring trained bears to defecate on his grave – Petros announces that he's dropping out of Med School.

At first I try to be rational about it by downing a bottle of gin, but then, caught in the wooziness, I'm overcome by a fiery wrath – the nerve of the little brat, throwing away everything his father and I have worked so hard for him to enjoy, wasting his life so he can play at being a writer with those god-awful books of his.

So, after his dad is done with him, it's my turn to protest, cursing him and calling him a monster. "That's what you've become! A monster!"

Whereupon Petros, tears welling in his eyes, replies: "It takes one to make one! If I'm a monster, then you're fucking Echidna!"

And then he leaves, slamming the door behind him.

And still staggering from the booze, I think of Echidna, that Mother of all Monsters, whose husband was a dragon buried under Mount Etna, and I remember Dad telling me how I looked like a fire-breathing dragon when I blew the cigarette smoke out my nostrils, and I can feel that mountain of guilt weighing upon me and trapping the fire in my insides, and I want to drink some more but first I must eat something, so I devour two family-size bags of crisps washed down with half a bottle of vodka and with twenty Valiums as a chaser; a couple of hours later Petros finds me unconscious on the living-room floor, covered in my own vomit.

With great effort he manages to drag me all the way to the bathroom, where he washes me like a baby, slaps my face to rouse me and, seeing I'm still lethargic, pinches my nose and forces me to swallow bubble bath, so I throw up a river of alcoholic bile and undigested pills. (Six months later, they'll find 220 of them in my stomach during the autopsy – that missing two, chasing me around.)

Then, after cleaning me up again, he drives me to the hospital to have my stomach pumped and undergo the necessary observation. The resident psychiatrist wants to admit me for the full 72-hour period required of him, but as soon as I come round I start crying and beg Petros not to leave me all alone in that place, promising I'll never do such a stupid thing again. So, after a couple of hours, the shrinks lets me go, after writing a prescription for, among other things, a drug called Tegretol, which Petros explains is an anticonvulsant.

"But I'm not epileptic," I say. Or am I? Could it be that everything I've been through all these years was the result of some kind of undiagnosed epilepsy?

"Some shrinks use them as mood stabilizers. I personally disagree, but let's just stick to the doctor's orders for the time being."

It would be such a pity if Petros really dropped out of Medical School. I can picture him as a therapist, curing people of their fears and their misery.

He might even be able to cure his old mum.

July

Tassos moves out.

The final straw is yet another fight, during which I rush to the balcony to jump to my death. Tassos, managing to grab me at the last moment, slaps some sense into me – the first time he's ever raised a hand to me. He's just saved my life, but I'm so mad at him, I say I'll make him pay for hitting me: one of these nights, when he's asleep, I'll pour boiling oil into his ear, or stab him in the neck and he'll be paralyzed for life and see who's helpless then.

And my poor sweet Eel gets so upset by the murderous glint in my eyes – and really, when you think about it, how could there be any guarantee I won't put my money where my mouth is? – that he suffers a hypertensive crisis.

Just then Petros walks into the room and, seeing his father collapsed on the sofa with eyes bulging and breath coming out in a rattle, takes his blood pressure and finds out to his horror that his diastolic pressure is nearly 120. So he helps him sit up and after Tassos repeats in a shaky voice what I've just threatened to do to him, Petros spits at me and packs a suitcase for his father, telling him to stay at his office for the foreseeable future.

"If you actually manage to kill him," he hisses at me while his dad's getting dressed, "don't expect me to stick around till you wear me out as well. I'll go away too and just leave you to rot."

I'm terrified. And there's no booze left in the house, I've drunk it all. I find only a half-bottle of red grappa, but the glass stopper is stuck and I can't wrench it loose no matter how I ache for the dark, ruby liquid and I can't very well ask Petros, who's still giving me a murderous look, to open it for me.

Tassos will never again spend a night at home as long as I live.

However, feeling wretchedly guilty for abandoning his duties as husband and father – for that is how he sees it, despite Petros's assurances that he's wrong, that he's done everything for us and now has to take care of himself and mind his health – he'll be dropping by every single day, laden with groceries and pills and money for both of us, so much money we don't know where to spend it. Whenever I need him, he's there.

Yet the next time he lies on our bed he'll be a widower.

August

One afternoon I come upon Petros smoking pot in his room and I go ballistic. So this is what we raised him like a prince for, so he could get stoned and end up an unemployed junkie begging in the streets for a hit?

Nowadays, however, my son doesn't raise his voice to me; he doesn't need to, he knows just the right thing to say.

"Like mother, like son. Go back to the living-room now and have a beer or ten to calm down. There's a good girl."

And as I softly close his bedroom door behind me, I feel the old wound opening up again.

He's right, after all. Do you recall the night of the quake, Katerina, when you polished off a bottle of whisky while you were still pregnant with Petros? Or when he was five and saw you writhing on the floor, so drunk and doped up you couldn't even sit up and hold him? It was a rare thing to see you sober.

He's right, you know, I think to myself while opening a bottle of tsipouro. I hate tsipouro, but it's the only bottle of alcohol left in the back of the cupboard. I ruined him myself. It's because of me that he's smoking weed, and if one of these days he tries heroin and crack and ends up homeless and dies from an overdose, it will be my fault.

And wishing to plunge into oblivion as fast as possible while at the same time sparing myself the hideous taste, I down the tsipouro in one gulp, as if it were water. Stupid.

The result: acute esophagitis.

So, once more, Petros has to nurse me back to health, feeding me strained peas and apple sauce and spoonfuls of warm milk.

One morning, weak from hunger and the Risperdal Dr Lemonis has prescribed, I don't make it to the bathroom on time and leave a trail of pee across the apartment.

Petros mops it up ungrudgingly. Isn't life just grand?

September - October

Petros is in love with someone from Athens. I don't even know if it's a girl or a guy, because he deliberately avoids using pronouns or other words that could reveal the gender – plus he almost never talks about this new '*love affair*' as he calls it without giving away any details. He knows I know, of course. He just wants to spare himself the added drama.

And one fine day he announces that he plans to go to Athens for a couple of weeks – business *and* pleasure, he adds. And it's only fair that I let him; he has to have at least some semblance of normality in his life, and love can't hurt.

But he's not asking my permission, I suddenly realize: it's a fait accompli.

So of course I have to take my own petty revenge at him and his father for leaving me all alone in the evenings, Tassos at his practice and Petros God knows where. That's what you want? Now you'll see.

And I go off my meds cold turkey for a whole week.

On the eighth day I wake up in complete derangement. Barefoot and wearing only a baggy T-shirt, I grab a crucifix and take to the streets, stopping people and telling them to kiss the crucifix because the end of the world is upon us.

(That is precisely what's happening inside me: my son is gone and my world is ending.)

Luckily, before I'm run over by a car, a neighbour spots me from the balcony and calls Tassos, who arrives along with the ambulance which will take me to a psychiatric clinic.

I'll remain there till the end of October, sometimes almost lucid and sometimes spaced out and unresponsive. On occasion, when Tassos comes to visit, I don't recognize him; I just feel this instinctive urge to trust him, so I ask him politely to help me escape from that place. Tassos weeps and I comfort him. "Don't cry, mister. Don't cry."

Petros also visits, when I'm having one of my good days, and I beg him too to help his poor mum and take me back home with him instead of leaving me there all alone in an empty white room.

Yet Tassos won't let me stay at home with the boy until he's certain I'm not a danger to myself or to Petros. To punish them, I just go off my antiepileptic pills, pretending to swallow them and then sticking them under the mattress, because I recall Petros saying they're not good for me, since I'm not epileptic.

The result, however, of this abrupt withdrawal is a violent grand mal seizure three days later. By the time Tassos arrives at the clinic, I've suffered another, and then two more in close succession, until my heart arrests and they have to use a defibrillator to resuscitate me.

After a while I regain my senses, but my mind has been shattered to pieces. When my son comes to see me, in the worst and most painful moment of his life, I smile at him as if he's a stranger, a childhood friend whose face I can't quite place. And when he tries to hold my hand, shedding silent tears, he sees that I am restrained with leather straps.

Petros will spend the following week hiding at a friend's place, his phone switched off, and his father looking for him frantically while I'm still lost in the dreamworld of antipsychotic stupor.

But in the end he'll come back home. Big mistake.

November - December

My life feels almost normal.

Tassos drops by every day, and he's especially attentive

towards me; sometimes he brings his laundry, and I load it into the washing machine, and I like it: it's as if we're a family again, even for as long as it takes to wash and iron a few shirts and socks. Plus, this is proof that there's no other woman in his life to take care of him. (How strange is this possessiveness. It lives on even when love is less than a faint memory.)

Petros goes out with a friend from high school at night and they usually stay out late and crash at home, where Manolis sleeps on the couch (since he lives out of town, plus he's fallen out with his parents). Sometimes, while my son is still sleeping, Manolis and I drink coffee and he tells me all about being gay, but he takes great care not to involve Petros in any of his narratives. Poor lambs. As if I care who sleeps with whom anymore.

Only one thing is occupying my mind these days: my plan.

I've had enough of the half-hearted attempts and the booze fests: now I'm hoarding pills, especially those I can get over the counter without a doctor's prescription – and anyhow, I've been on so many different kinds of meds all these years that no one really knows what my prescribed dosage is (I'm not even sure of it myself) and it's easy to save them up, while at the same time I give my shrink the impression that all's well and no bad thoughts are crossing my mind.

This time no one will manage to find me early enough and pull me out of the sack. I'll make sure of it.

I'll choose the day carefully, knowing that Tassos will be away in Athens at a conference and Petros will be at his high-school reunion that'll probably last an entire night and then some.

December 27. My last morning coffee.

The Last Day

I am serene; almost happy. But why?

Because today I'm giving Petros the biggest gift within my powers: I shall release him from the lifelong duty of nursing a mother who's constantly deteriorating, spare him the years of dementia that are sure to come, and liberate him from a life spent in solitude and loss, so as to fill up the desert of my own non-life. I am fully conscious of my intended actions: I know this will destroy him, that he'll need years and years to recovers from the blow, but time flies and after a while the pain will ebb away and vanish and my son will be, at long last, free.

Petros wakes up at noon. I fix him his breakfast, trying not to think it's the last time I pamper him.

We spend the afternoon and most of the evening together, listening to music. I want my last hours to be filled with music, immersed in song.

We listen to a lot of Leonard Cohen's cold and broken hallelujahs, and then I ask Petros to play me that song 'Annabel Lee', and manage not to shed a single tear.

Does he know? I wonder. Can he sense what is going on underneath my veil of tranquillity? Perhaps.

Because, right before he heads out to meet his old friends, he takes the supermarket disposable camera he's bought for the reunion, and snaps a photo of me.

My last photo will be blurry.

I'll kiss him goodbye for the last time, tell him to drive carefully, and listen to some more music on my own, this time letting myself cry for all the things I'm about to lose in a matter of hours. What I don't lose is my nerve.

This time I'm not drinking any alcohol: I can't risk being sick and ruining it.

Between ten and twelve I will ingest (according to Petros's calculation, picking up all the empty pill boxes and bottles the following morning) roughly four hundred pills.

And just before my head begins to spin, I'll take a piece of paper and a light blue Magic Marker (where did you come from? What childhood washed you up and into my hands on this very night?) and write a farewell note to Petros. Then, dragging my feet back to the bedroom, I'll fold the paper and place it inside a matchbox, which I'll then stick in an old boot at the back of the closet, as if I don't want him to find it. (He will, months later.)

And then I undress and lie down.

I am serene. Almost happy.

And the Lights Will Shine Brightly

I wish you have children someday, so that you can love them as much as I loved you, and be loved by them as much as you loved me.

These will be my parting words to Petros, written on that folded-up piece of paper in that matchbox.

And then? Then, in the dead of the night, something will flutter inside me: my little nothing ready to fly away and join the great, big nothing.

Or hoping to find itself in a life as glorious as the one I'm leaving behind.

Fly, Little Katerina.

PARTHIAN TRANSLATIONS

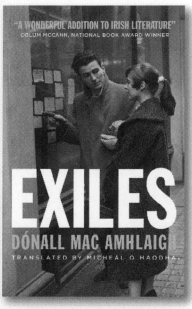

EXILES

Dónall Mac Amhlaigh

Translated from Irish
by Mícheál Ó hAodha

Out October 2020

£12.00
978-1-912681-31-0

HANA

Alena Mornštajnová

Translated from Czech
by Julia and Peter Sherwood

Out October 2020

£10.99
978-1-912681-50-1

Creative Europe

LA BLANCHE

Maï-Do Hamisultane

Translated from French
by Suzy Ceulan Hughes

£8.99
978-1-912681-23-5

THE NIGHT CIRCUS
AND OTHER STORIES

Uršuľa Kovalyk

Translated from Slovak
by Julia and Peter Sherwood

£8.99
978-1-912681-04-4

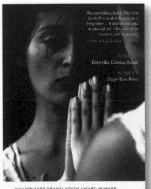

A GLASS EYE

Miren Agur Meabe

Translated from Basque
by Amaia Gabantxo

£8.99
978-1-912109-54-8

PARTHIAN TRANSLATIONS

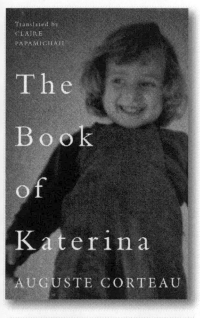

THE BOOK OF KATERINA

Auguste Corteau

Translated from Greek by Claire Papamichail

Out 2021

£10.00
978-1-912681-26-6

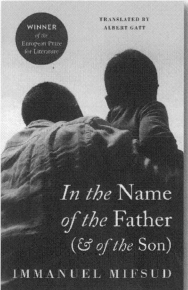

IN THE NAME OF THE FATHER (& OF THE SON)

Immanuel Mifsud

Translated from Maltese by Albert Gatt

£6.99
978-1-912681-30-3

Creative Europe

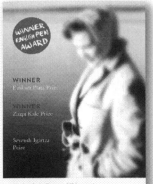

HER MOTHER'S HANDS

Karmele Jaio

Translated from Basque
by Kristin Addis

£8.99
978-1-912109-55-5

WOMEN WHO
BLOW ON KNOTS

Ece Temelkuran

Translated from Turkish
by Alexander Dawe

£9.99
978-1-910901-69-4

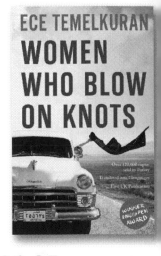

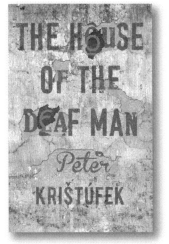

THE HOUSE OF
THE DEAF MAN

Peter Krištúfek

Translated from Slovak
by Julia and Peter Sherwood

£11.99
978-1-909844-27-8

PARTHIAN TRANSLATIONS

DEATH DRIVES AN AUDI

Kristian Bang Foss

Winner of the European Prize for Literature

£10.00
978-1-912681-32-7

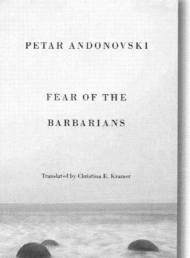

FEAR OF BARBARIANS

Petar Adonovski

Winner of the European Prize for Literature

£9.00
978-1-913640-19-4

Creative Europe

PARTHIAN TRANSLATIONS

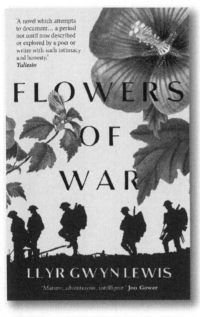

FLOWERS OF WAR

Llyr Gwyn Lewis

Short-Listed for Wales
Book of the Year

———

£9.00
978-1-912681-25-9

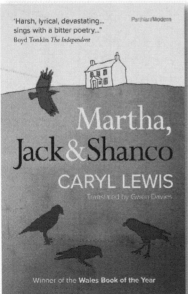

MARTHA, JACK AND SHANCO

Caryl Lewis

Winner of the Wales
Book of the Year

Out October 2020

———

£9.99
978-1-912681-77-8

Creative
Europe